THE ART OF WORK
PHAYE POLIAKOFF-CHEN

CW01095396

booktrope

Booktrope Editions
Seattle, Washington, USA, 2013

Edited by Rachel Brookhart

Cover Design by Julia Kim Smith

This is a work of fiction. Names, characters, places, brands, media, and incidents are either the product of the author's imagination or are used fictitiously. Any resemblance to similarly named places or to persons living or deceased is unintentional.

PAPERBACK ISBN 978-1-935961-92-5
EPUB ISBN 978-1-62015-096-2

For further information regarding permissions, please contact info@booktrope.com.

Library of Congress Control Number: 2013933055

For Allen, Elliot, and Matthew

In Memory of Kelly Dalla Tezza

"The Javon" originally appeared in *Praxilla,* Spring 2009.

Contents

Acknowledgments

I am indebted to the many people who fostered this manuscript, especially Charles Johnson, David Bosworth, David Downing, Kelly Causey, Marianne Connolly, Kari Hanson, and my patient and supportive family. I am grateful to Julia Kim Smith for her artful cover design. Special thanks to Kenneth Shear, Rachel Brookhart, and Jesse James Freeman of Booktrope.

The Javon

My father was shrinking. A man who had shouted and paced in courtrooms was now connected to a canister of oxygen and a clear bag of fluid that dripped into the back of his hand. The problem was, I had nothing to say. I sat in the hospital and tried to think of what lasting impressions I wanted to have, what profound matters we should be discussing, but I couldn't think. I felt like I was on a long trip and had forgotten to pack something important, but I couldn't remember what.

My father's only advice, given every time he saw me, was, "Drive carefully."

I always responded the same way: "No, Daddy, I'm going to drive like a javon." It was our family tradition to answer every command sarcastically, as if we were all above receiving any instructions. Driving like a javon meant driving so fast that the air blurred into the scenery, and so recklessly that other cars pulled off the road and pedestrians dove into ditches. The police had no chance in the chase. A javon was an exotic muscular bird, a slim jaguar with wings.

His hospital room was white tinged with green. I liked the starkness of the sheets, how crisp they were compared to the wrinkly things I had grown up sleeping on. The family made sure that his room not look sterile. We cluttered it up so much with our magazines and bottles of possible remedies, it looked like the house he'd left behind. The nightstand was jumbled with greeting cards and hopeful books, aspirin, vitamins, and chewing gum. The yertzite candle he had lit for his mother had long since burned out, and the wax still clung to the sides of the glass. In an effort to tidy up, a nurse had begun filling it with the loose change from around the room. He'd asked that we bring him a yarmulke, and every so often he put it on and prayed, but I never thought to ask for what. Sometimes I listened to the cadence of the Hebrew, old words comforting like lullabies.

My job was fixing meals, making sure he avoided the jaundiced hospital meals of lemon Jell-O and leathery fish.

"Ready for supper, Daddy?"

"Just about."

I think he was never hungry then; he just liked the assurance of a schedule. Certainly he was never hungry for the food I fixed: brown

rice and black beans, steamed broccoli and carrots in bright, day-
glo colors, and sauces made of peanuts and peppers. I believed in
that food. I read of miracle cures of faith and health food, and since
the surgery had left him weaker and short a lung, he pretended to
believe in it also, probably as a favor to me. I carted armfuls of plastic
containers to the hospital every day, and spread them out on the
counter of the visitors' kitchen where I prepared the meals before an
audience. Emaciated men in baggy, striped pajamas and fat women
in pink bathrobes glared at my lunches.

"You oughta fix your Daddy some steak."

"Maybe so," I'd say, glaring back, convinced I was saving him from
being poisoned.

I carried the food back to the room, though he never ate all of it.
When he finished, I rinsed the dishes in the bathroom sink where
the water was never hot enough to get them clean. They stayed
greasy, and the bits of food left in the sink made me gag. I closed
my eyes as I turned the water on full blast, guiding the food down
the drain.

I sat in the green vinyl chair beside my father's bed and looked out
the window onto the parking lot. I could see the heat waves rising off
my car; I'd driven like a javon to get there in time for supper. It took
my body a while to settle into the hospital quiet.

"Get you anything?"

"No thanks."

I wanted to make him talk. But I could never find the thread that
would begin one of his stories. Sometimes his old cronies came in,
and one lead-in line could get him rolling for an hour or two, but they
came by less the weaker and smaller he got, and I had never known
the secret to starting him up.

I brought books, but I never read. Being in the hospital made me
feel like I was in the doctor's office waiting room, so that I could only
concentrate on magazines. I flipped through a women's magazine
– bright pictures of casseroles and babies, and implausible human
interest stories. Here was a woman who landed a plane after her
husband not only had a heart attack at the controls, but fell over on
top of her as she was trying to bring them both to safety. Here was a
holiday dinner you could make in less than five minutes.

"It's time for the news," my father reminded me. That was our
pattern, and I was always relieved to turn the news on for us. I sank
down into the vinyl chair and the steady drone of the news voice
calmed me, finally brought my pulse all the way down to a flat,
quiet rate.

Here was a dog that rescued an infant from the second floor of a burning house. Here was the diet plan of the stars.

When the news ended, an ancient rerun of The Real McCoys came on. We listened to the theme song begin: "I want you to meet a family, known as the Real McCoys." I wanted to turn it off, but I was stuck to my chair; my father made no effort to press the remote control switch. Through the air conditioning vent above we could hear the hum of the TV in the room upstairs. "From West Virginny they came to stay/ In sunny Californ-I-Ay...."

A grainy image of Walter Brennan appeared on the screen. He was limping as always. I wondered then if Walter Brennan was dead. I turned around to ask my father, but he was watching the screen intently. Whenever either of us started watching something, no matter how bad, we had to stick around for the end.

Walter Brennan had decided to sue his neighbors for a million dollars. Something about a cow.

"That's legally incorrect, isn't it Daddy?"

"Not much of a case."

Walter Brennan lost his case. There was a moral at the end – don't sue for a million dollars, lock the gate after your cows. Walter limped off the screen, and I thought maybe I could ask my father about his cases, if maybe he worried about someone else taking them over, but he had fallen asleep. The commercials started – a water-logged diaper that didn't drip, another dinner to make in just under five minutes. I turned off the TV quickly before another program could start.

I dozed in my chair like I was in the passenger seat on a long car ride; it was a sleep troubled by dreams. I was walking the halls, looking for a nurse. There was no nurse. I was heating his lunch and it wouldn't get hot. There was no five minute lunch.

I think that my father swallowed his coughs and kept quiet during my shifts. Both my mother and brother spoke of getting up eight or ten times to help him through coughing fits and seizures. At most, I would get up once or twice to shuffle down the hall for the nurse. Yet when I woke up, we both looked haggard.

"Daddy, I'd like to run some errands. Will you be okay until Mom gets here?"

"Sure, drive carefully."

"No, I'm going to drive like a javon." I was almost out the door when I turned to him, and asked suddenly, "Say, what is a javon anyway?"

"You mean Jay Vaughn."

"What?"

"Jay Vaughn Hutto, client of mine. A race car driver from around here – never made it real big. Once he got drunk and led the police in circles around the parking lot at the fair grounds. He almost did time for that one. I got him off because back then, you couldn't get arrested for reckless driving on private property." My father chuckled, "One of those policemen gave me a speeding ticket every chance he got after that. Old Jay Vaughn."

I light the yerzite candle for him each year, and the ritual puts me at ease. When the candle burns out, I scrape away the leftover wax and use the glass for juice.

I still drive like a javon. Sometimes when I'm speeding down a dark highway and letting the motel signs turn into blurs of neon even though I'm exhausted, I think of the time when I was in the fifth grade and my brother was in junior high, that we went on a long car trip with my parents. Late one night, we were lost off a confusing cloverleaf of highways, looking for the Howard Johnson's. We pulled over and asked a man we saw by the side of the road for help. He staggered to the window – I'll never forget his yellow eyes or the stench of his breath.

"How do you get to the Howard Johnson's?" we asked.

"Howard Who?" he yelled back.

I insist this happened in Baltimore, my mother says Atlanta, my brother says in the mountains near Knoxville. I'm sure my father would have known.

The Art of Work

When the Mexican migrant worker told Norah that she wasn't a damn revolutionary, it bothered her. Because she thought she was. She had been hired to raise money for migrant workers' families, and she thought the job gave her credibility. But when he told her she had none, she had to accept that it was a job she had just shrugged on, like a scrap of cloth. All of Norah's jobs were that way, a covering of sorts. She pieced them together, not relying on any one to represent who she was or wasn't, as her migrant worker told her. So when another job came along - modeling for an artist — to supplement, to give her another layer, she accepted.

She'd known Gina for ages, though never very well. Their paths would cross when Gina designed posters for whatever cause was most crucial — whatever cause that would get the most press, in Norah's opinion. Norah had never really trusted Gina, but she liked the harshness of her art work.

Gina stood in the entry of the hollow apartment, looking at Norah in the same careful way she did when Norah asked her for money for the migrant workers. Gina motioned her in with a tilt of her head, brushing black curls out of her eyes.

"Coffee, Norah." A statement.

"Yes please. Black." Norah answered just as shortly, fearing that words would distract her.

But it didn't seem to matter. Gina babbled on quickly as she led Norah inside. The smells were nauseating — cat box, wet dog, turpentine, and oil paint — until she forced herself to breathe through her mouth.

"This is actually where Thomas lives; we share the workspace," said Gina. Thomas stood in the back of the loft, adjusting the shades on the windows, playing with the available light.

Norah modeled on a rickety platform surrounded by easels and animals. She counted four cats and three dogs who modeled with her, pacing when she moved, settling down as she sank into her pose. Norah's first pose was easy — legs draped over a nubby green sofa cushion, weight resting on her forearms. What was hard was keeping herself occupied internally. If her mind drifted, would her body drift as well? Even though the loft was cold, and she was very still, the hot coffee made her shake and sweat. She could feel the long lines of sweat running from armpit to thigh, but she wasn't allowed to turn her head to see or rub it away. The sounds of an argument distracted her from her predicament.

"Thomas, you think your poverty makes you better, but your nobility is dull," Gina said out of the blue, not looking at Thomas or Norah, but brushing eraser gum from her canvas.

Norah's precarious relationship with money made her hate arguments about it. "Nice animals," she said.

Gina stepped back and looked at her work. "Oh, that's Thomas's way of bringing his work home. He has to remind us that his money is unrelated to his art."

"I work at an animal shelter," Thomas said. "A 'kill' animal shelter."

"He's a fickle god — saving some, carrying others to the ovens."

"We don't use ovens anymore," Thomas said. "We use needles," he demonstrated in the air, pushing in an imaginary plunger then snapping his ruddy fingers. "It's over like that."

"How do you decide?" Norah asked.

"Fate," he said.

Norah let it drop and turned her head slightly to watch Gina work. Her smock was really a faded karate gi, which she wore sashed with the long sleeves of an old cardigan, letting the threadbare black sweater flop in the back. The gi was stained with streaks of paint, long since washed and dried into the weave of the fabric. She wore nothing on her long pale legs, as if she were wearing a robe and had just stepped out of bed. They leaned over their easels; Gina stared at the space that Norah defined, and Thomas stared at Norah.

Nudity was an armor, Norah knew, fooling people into thinking you were giving up more of yourself than you were. Even though she wasn't especially skinny, she wasn't afraid to undress. She worked as a live nude girl once, literally twisting scarves around herself and whispering to men, "Got a quarter for the juke box? I'll dance for you." She didn't last long — the smoke and the hands got to her after a while. But there was a part of her that believed that when she danced, she was finally working honestly — that she was selling sex openly instead of implicitly when waiting tables or typing letters. Modeling would maybe be the same as dancing, only elite — working for art, instead of putting one over on some men at a bar.

Norah imagined strata of working naked. Modeling for artists, that would be on the top rung; dancing in a bar was a few rungs down, and, she thought, fucking was always last.

The loud metal click of a paint box closing startled her.

"I need to get to work," Thomas was saying. "Some of us don't sell out our art."

Gina didn't look up, but recited her line: "I wish you would stop."

"Never," he said.

"I can understand," Norah said. "Sometimes getting paid for what you love can ruin it for you." She held her pose, not turning her head, so she couldn't see if Thomas smiled.

"Gina - come by the shelter. There's a dumb old lab you'll like," he said as he left. He didn't say goodbye to Norah.

Gina waited until Thomas was out the door before she put her charcoal down. "I have a gallery opening soon - I have some ideas I'd like to try with you," she said. Gina dragged a basket of old clothes and blankets to the platform. Norah sat on the edge while Gina draped layers of quilts and petticoats around her, standing back, then draping more on.

"When is your opening?"

"In a couple months. We have time."

Norah stopped talking to let Gina concentrate. "We'll try this," she said, arranging a white sheet starkly in the center, which she twisted to hide the rips and stains. Norah folded her body to match the curve of the sheet and waited.

"Good," she said.

"Do you and Thomas argue all the time?"

"It helps pass the time. We seem to argue more when my shows open."

Norah scratched a three-legged dog behind the ears. "It seems like it's your way of flirting."

"With Thomas?" Gina knitted her thick eyebrows. "No. You're wrong."

"I'm sorry," she finally said. "I just think there are better things to argue about than money."

"There are no better things to argue about."Gina flicked a speck of paint off her gi. "You're not still working for the migrants, are you Norah?"

"Some. Though I do feel useless stuffing envelopes and whining for money. You're lucky you can donate your art."

"Lucky? I wouldn't call it luck at all." Gina breathed sharply out her nose. "Speaking of money, what do you say to strangers when you canvass? That the farm workers are exploited?"

"Something like that."

"No, what words do you use — exploited or oppressed?"

"Neither."

"Admit it. You go around repeating some rote prose."

"Christ," Norah said. "I work for a commission. I say whatever you want. Why are you so worked up about it?"

"Because it's important. We all argue about money. You just do it for a living. Argument by coercion or sentimentality is still argument. What kind of commission do you make?"

"That's the problem. Not much. It's hard being broke while raising money for other people."

During the next modeling sessions, she studied their paintings as a way to understand both Gina and Thomas. The pieces on the walls were different from their working canvases; it would have been impossible to tell that the original background was a splintery platform covered with rags in a sooty loft. The revisions must have been made in some secret place, away from the original inspiration.

Gina had her own ideas about what Norah looked like. She enlarged parts of her, embellishing with lace and shades of purple and green. Mug-shot photographs of arms and legs blended into her giant screens. The pieces she had hung on the walls had the flavor of her arguments — abrupt and spiky. Gina's paintings were at odds with one another. Her style was elusive, whereas Thomas stuck with a bright style, a cross between Van Gogh and Peter Max. It made him seem simple to Norah. And as much as he complained about working in the animal shelter, it was part of him, reflected in his art, down to the dog hairs embedded in the paint.

One thing about Thomas, though: he always made Norah look sexy. He gave her a big butt, rounded out her breasts, and ignored the various scars — the bike wreck, the appendectomy. He made her pubic hair even; Thomas airbrushed her as he went. Norah never felt she could recognize herself in his work.

Norah was in a peculiar pose of Thomas's choice - feet perched on a coffee table, toes pointed, and her body twisted over the sofa.

"Thomas, that is the ugliest pose I've ever seen you design," Gina said. She left her easel and paced. "Norah, you must be miserable."

"Thanks," she laughed. "I'd like to move my hand if that's okay." Her left hand was numb from the wrist down, so she had to use her right hand to lift it and to shake it. As the feeling returned, she groaned.

"Would you mind keeping that pose — just for a little longer?" Thomas asked. "It's important to me."

"Sure," Norah said. As soon as she put her hand down again, it became dead weight.

"I can't work with this," Gina said. "I have to go to the gallery anyway. They said I could go in today and start putting the show up." When Gina left, Thomas offered Norah more coffee.

"No thanks," she said, sure of herself. "Don't you and Gina ever work together without arguing?"

"Not really," Thomas said. "It keeps my heart pounding so I can work."

"I just realized: me too. It might be harder to sit still otherwise." It was just the opposite in canvassing — one argument would ruin a whole day. She'd feel so defensive afterward, no one would give her money. Norah tried to concentrate on the pose. One of the cats kneaded its claws into her back, with just enough pressure to tickle and too little to actually make her move him. She enjoyed the challenge of staying still.

Thomas was looking between Norah and his easel as if he were watching a tennis game. Finally he spoke. "I've always wanted to ask you, Norah, what do you *think* about when you work? You're always so still, so perfect. What do you *think* about?"

"Thomas, I think about sex." A half-true flirtation. She could see Thomas try to hide a smile. Modeling was acting, but then so was working in an office. But no one ever asked her what she thought about when she filed tax receipts. She had become a good model because she was able to hold a creative pose, and she did it by thinking about sex, any scene from her past, until it took a life of its own: another sort of airbrushing, no awkward pantyhose or twisted bras, instead simple, erotic recreations.

When her time was up, she went into the back bedroom to change as usual. It would have felt like a strip show if she had taken off her clothes in their workspace. Instead, she came to work dressed in frumpy jeans and baggy t-shirts and changed in the bedroom into a soft cotton robe. At the end of the sessions, she returned to the bedroom in her robe and dressed in there with the door closed.

Thomas was standing in the hallway in front of a print of Gina's when Norah opened the door. Gina's signature in the right hand corner was in an unexpectedly loopy, childishly legible script. The piece was intricately framed — glass over a beige mat, over a green mat, surrounded by a green metal frame. The watercolor beneath was dreamy and languid, deceptively sweet at first glance, but just this side of surreal; the nude woman blended into the background of the painting, so that it was hard to tell where the boundaries of flesh and cloth were.

Thomas stared at Norah, and then they kissed hard. Damn, she thought, but kept on kissing him. Thomas put his tongue so far down her throat that she had to breathe in sharply. He stood beside her and lifted her shirt slightly. They could see themselves in the reflection of the painting. Thomas slipped one arm around her and waved his palm over her nipple, letting his fingers find the outside curve of her breast. He looked not at Norah, but at their reflections, and the way the reflections were superimposed over the nude Gina had painted.

"You have nice arms," Norah told him.

"It's from lifting dead dogs." Thomas said.

They stood still for a moment, his hands resting on her breasts, her shirt pulled up to her collar bone, her head tilted to one side. "I'd ask you to stay," Thomas said, "but fucking your model is such a cliché."

Norah walked to the gallery that housed Gina's opening along streets that were lined with garbage. Broken trash bags had sat for weeks because of a strike, the seams ripped open by rats and age, spilling bits of lunches, paper towels. The roofs must have been full of the garbage too, because as the wind picked up, it all whipped through the air, like autumn leaves. The garbage men had been on strike for weeks now, and as hard as Norah tried to sympathize, she hated the way they left the whole city hanging, stubbing toes on the bags of trash, ducking the napkins and coffee-stained paper cups that rained down, while well-fed rats dove like merry children into the sewers.

Inside, the gallery walls were white; lights beamed down from ceiling tracks. Norah realized that the lights were shining on enlarged parts of her body in Gina's paintings. It was disarming, so she headed first for the table in the middle of the floor, where wine glasses were arranged in formation, rows of red and white wine already poured so no one would see the cheap bottles. As she sipped the awful sweet wine, she felt Thomas whisper in her ear.

"When the strike is over, they can come pick up these things on the walls." Thomas smiled.

"Jealous, now," she said. "That's not nice." She brushed his cheek with her lips.

"It's just such a waste of a model." Thomas said as he pulled her by the elbow to the edge of the room.

Across the room, in front of a large canvas, Gina was holding court. Dressed in a tight black shift, she laughed and tilted her chin to the ceiling. Norah studied her reflection in the glass frame of a lacy painting. Gina looked like a painting of an artist enjoying attention, and Norah tried to share her glory secretly.

As she watched Gina, Thomas reappeared with more wine that they drank together, the substance too thin to get drunk on without company.

"I want to see Gina's masterpiece, Thomas. She seems to be thriving in front of it." She moved across the room to the crowd around Gina. The conversations around her blended together with the clinking of glasses and grew louder as she reached Gina. Behind her, a realistic painting filled the back wall. "I'm moving toward super-realism," Gina was saying to a critic. "I find it somehow cheerful."

Norah stood stunned before it. It was a life-size portrait of her. The only one in the room that was an exact likeness, it had captured an expression that she thought she had learned to hide — her face contorted in an angry scowl. She'd tried to hide that expression since she'd seen it in the mirror in junior high. At her groin were three vaginas. In the right hand corner Gina's loopy scrawl looked out of place - it belonged on a nursery illustration.

Quickly she turned to Gina. "Congratulations, love," she said. Just as quickly, she tried to disappear into the crowd. As hard as she tried to convince herself that no one could recognize her, she could feel her cheeks grow warm.

This was more than nudity. It was as if Gina had taped a page of her diary to the canvas and dotted the page with forgeries. She continued her patterned walk along the walls, stopping at each piece as if she were studying it, but she kept stealing glances at the painting on the back wall. All of a sudden, Thomas appeared in her line of vision.

"It bothers you, doesn't it?"

"How did you know?"

"I've seen that look — when a model recognizes something in herself in Gina's paintings."

"I didn't think it was there to recognize, is all."

"Not that it matters. Her paintings aren't about the models. She works on the larger picture." Thomas turned to Norah, blocking the painting with his body.

She was afraid she might believe him and take him home with her, so she walked outside instead and leaned against the building. Had there been a naked workers' local, she would have gone on strike.

She draped her sweater around her shoulders and started walking. It was too late in the evening to find another job, but she thought she might find some hint. A few blocks ahead, rows of X-rated movie posters papered the buildings.   Strings of Xs described the movies; evidently, the more the better, like high school love notes — xoxoxo, Norah.   She looked closely at the faces on the ads, but their expressions told her nothing.   She walked on, hoping to find a migrant worker around, a reader of oracles who might tell her what she wasn't.

In the Sub-Basement of the Purple Zone

Richard's classroom was in the sub-basement of the purple zone in the south end of the hospital. To get there he had to circle the zones – white to yellow to red to purple — then dip down four flights of stairs below the ground. He could not take the elevator, could not prepare himself for the scene the elevator doors would open onto: someone on a stretcher, shaved head or head wrapped in bandages, bottles of transparent liquids dripping into their arms. He watched them cradling their pain. If he saw someone, leg raised in an inhuman angle in traction, his own knee would ache, the muscles pulled taut into place; if he saw someone with a wrapped head, he could feel the bandages tightening around his own skull.

When he opened the door to the sub-basement, he came face-to-face with the sign: "WARNING! ASBESTOS AREA RESTRICTED DO NOT ENTER THIS HALLWAY WITHOUT APPROPRIATE PROTECTION." He responded with a sad laugh: most of his students, and most everyone else who worked down here couldn't read well enough to understand that sign. There was too much to teach them.

His class, the maids and janitors of the hospital, waited for him, assembled around the splintered conference table. All of them were black; Richard felt his whiteness intensely each afternoon. They were smoking cigarettes, even though Richard had politely asked them not to. He stopped making a fuss over it, and prepared his lungs for their smoke.

"Mr. Richard," Pearl yelled to him, "you remember now about our Thanksgiving party, right? You can just show up, no need for you to worry about cooking."

But he'd planned on cooking. Did they not think him capable or was she being polite? "Of course I remember, Pearl. But I'll cook too." Richard blushed as he smiled. Trying to hide how grateful he was for the invitation, he changed the subject. "Isn't it your turn today for book reports?"

Pearl stood up from the table, a ritual from the fourth grade when she was last in school. Richard had sorted his students by ability. Most of them sat at the conference table with Pearl, but he had managed to find desks for the strongest and the weakest. All fourteen of them were crammed into the same windowless room; Richard tried to divide his time among them.

Pearl wiped her hands on the front of her polyester pants, already stained with soap and dirt on two shiny lines down the thighs. She had picked a Harlequin romance and was holding up the jacket cover – a white family in a covered wagon being chased by a band of screaming, half-naked Indians.

"Where does this take place?" Richard asked.

"Oklahoma?"

"You tell me."

"I guess Oklahoma."

"Let's stop for a second. Where is Oklahoma?"

Richard was never prepared for the silence that followed a question like that. Did it matter where Oklahoma was?

"North Carolina?" asked Pamela.

"No." Sorry, he wanted to add, like an emcee on a game show.

He drew a map of the Untied States like a giant inflatable letter H on the chalk board. He drew an X about where Oklahoma was, and then placed an X on North Carolina, for home. Born on the floors above and pushed down to the sub-basement. And then, beyond that, the map was anybody's guess. One of the floor sweepers carefully wrote the word Japan where Mexico should have been.

"Let's move on." Richard made a note to include a geography lesson at some point. Would it be before or after the lesson on asbestos poisoning or the conjugation of forms of to be, or how to read a paycheck stub? Maybe it didn't matter; at this point, New York, Tennessee, may as well have been Japan.

Pearl read another passage from her book.

"This part here, this is where they gets attacked by the Pueblos," she pronounced it Pew Blows, "and the Navajos." She gave the j a harsh sound.

"That's 'pwayblow' and 'nahvaho'. Do you know who they are?"

She squinched her eyes up for a minute, pursed her lips, and was silent. She tried to out-wait Richard, but he stood patiently.

Finally she asked, "Are they Jews?"

"Warning," Richard thought, flashing on the asbestos sign. "No, they're not Jews. They are Indians, Native Americans."

He paused, and then asked in an up-beat voice, "Why would we call them Native Americans?"

Everyone was silent except for Edna Martin, their only class member who was working on high school material, who turned around from her corner to face the class. She whacked her history book to get their attention.

"They were born here," Edna said. "Before the white folk, before the black folk. And the only reason that we call them Indians is because when the fool white folk got here, they thought they were in India, thought they were thousands of miles from where they were." The release of their laughter eased the tension for a moment, and Edna leaned over her workbook again.

Richard squeezed between the conference table and the desks so he could reach Mr. Rowe, who sat in an opposite corner of the room. Mr. Rowe was the farthest behind – he couldn't read at all. Richard had started him on his alphabet in the spring. Now he had advanced to making up words. Richard had had no earthly idea how to teach him. He liked the old man, and out of respect he called him Mr. Rowe, not Bernard. He gave him an exercise for the day: "Think of as many words as you can that rhyme with man. And then words that rhyme with okay." Mr. Rowe sat in the corner with an alphabet in front of him, trying out every letter – ban, can, dan, ean...bay, cay, day. Mr. Rowe pronounced the written words carefully, as if he were speaking a foreign language.

"Mr. Richard, I got the idea, now," Mr. Rowe told him, forcing Richard back to the larger group.

Pamela's turn. Pamela was just on the verge of making it into high school, so that she could spend the hours in the corners, like Edna, working in the high school workbooks, until she got her degree. She talked about the event of getting the degree as magic. Richard worked with two distinct goals: one was to enlighten and provide insight; the other was for them to get better jobs. The two goals battled one another for importance. He tried to plan assignments that would involve both goals, but it was often futile. The two goals were entirely different. He could not tell them yet that the diploma might only open the door to frustrations they hadn't dreamed of. Everyone was trying to catch up to Edna Martin and her high school workbooks, but she was in the same place as everyone else. He could explain about asbestos dust danger, but there was no way to reverse the effects of ten or twenty years of exposure.

Richard had given Pamela *Native Son*.

"This is just some civil rights shit," she said, and sat back down.

Richard shrugged, not knowing what else to say. As a white man, he couldn't respond to the depths of her cynicism. It wasn't his place to say that her attitude was too bitter.

"Pamela, you have to try harder than that. At least tell us why next time."

Pamela glanced over at Pearl, and Richard broke the silence, "Well, I guess it's time. Are there any questions, comments before we break?" No one spoke. The women were already standing, moving toward their carts loaded down with toilet paper and pink cleaning fluid. The hospital gave them a room, and just enough time to learn that they didn't know anything.

That night, at home, Richard prepared his dish for the Thanksgiving party. He wanted to make something special, elegant, but not too different. He had bought the ingredients the day before, and had arranged them on his refrigerator shelf.

"Looks like somebody lives here," he said when he opened the door, letting the cold air make him shiver as he admired his work. Usually, the fridge was empty except for the bag of coffee in the corner, the jar of jam that had a teaspoon of pale orange gel left in it, and eleven eggs, bought when Martha came back for a night.

He'd met her when he had been an organizer against the death penalty. She was one of his best volunteers – gathering signatures, knocking on doors for money. She had led a letter-writing campaign to the power company – telling them that she was deducting the cost of running the electric chair from her power bill each month. When Richard quit the death penalty, she fell in love with the migrant farm worker organizer who worked in the office down the hall.

He took twenty-four new potatoes, brushed them with oil, set them in the oven on a bed of rock salt for forty-five minutes.

He thought about Mr. Rowe mouthing sounds. Teaching by the seat of his pants. Edna could go on her own, she hardly needed him; she knew that material better than he did. And Mr. Rowe, well, Richard was going to find him a tutor soon enough – someone who knew what to do. Richard could defend his rhyming exercises, but teaching in general still baffled him. He had spent many years at Citizens Against the Death Penalty, raising money, writing inspired pamphlets — "educating," as his co-workers called it. ("Educating" as opposed to "teaching.") *Why do we kill to show that killing is wrong?*

He wished that had been his phrase – he had used it all the time. He went to teaching when it became impossible for him to work against capital punishment.

At Citizens Against the Death Penalty, he was always writing one more rushed plea. Every time an execution was scheduled, Richard's job was to write an impassioned letter, a call for an organized protest. The final plea he was assigned to write was to save William Moss' life.

But when he read about Moss' crimes in the newspaper, he couldn't write it. Moss had murdered two teenagers – stuffed them in a truck, rode around with them for a few hours, left them in the woods, then came back and raped the dead girl. As Richard had read about it in the paper, the first though he had was, "Let that man die." He could not imagine standing in front of the state prison, in the cold dark, holding a candle in an all night vigil for this man. He did not want to write a plea for other people to stand outside for this man at midnight. Let that man die.

The vigil happened anyway, the night before Moss' execution. Richard didn't write the letter for Moss, and didn't stand in the cold, holding a candle or leading the group of those holding candles in song. He had waited a few weeks before he quit, until he found this job teaching. It was a new program, in-house adult education, something that the hospital administrators could make themselves feel good about. It served the same purpose for Richard.

It had been plausible for him to leave the death penalty job, though he never told anyone, not even Martha, his real reasons. He was leaving for just another movement job at movement wages.

He sliced the potatoes in half, dropped them in hot oil, frying them until crisp. Did it matter if they could conjugate the verb to be? He knew it sounded arbitrary to them; they couldn't remember how to do it.

"The mens be bringing something to the Thanksgiving party, too. Not just the womens be cooking." That was correct to them, and now it seemed almost correct to Richard.

He scooped out the white potato insides; put them in a bowl with some sour cream. He lined up the fried skins on a big tray, carefully spooned enough of their dressed-up innards into each one. The recipe called for a topping of caviar. Richard decided that was too fancy, so he prepared small pieces of bacon instead. When he had finished, he had a military tray of potatoes – six rows, eight potatoes deep, each with a red stripe on top.

The party was in the clinic waiting room in the white zone, near where Richard parked. Each day, on his way to the purple zone, Richard gave the white zone a wide berth because it housed the oncology clinic. Most of the people who waited there stared at the reception desk, stared resentfully at every healthy person who walked through. Their bandages were usually clean, small, and square, but Richard imagined too vividly what lay underneath. Emaciated, with perhaps a few tufts of hair, radiation ports outlined in magic marker in inhuman geometric shapes on their bodies, they terrified him, like denizens of a world after nuclear war.

He felt their ghosts, even though Housekeeping and Laundry had transformed the white zone waiting area by setting up long tables in the middle of the room and covering them with industrial white table cloths that were stiff and hung awkwardly over the edges of the tables.

Everyone brought food: Pamela brought her lima bean stew – lima beans simmered in water and fatback for days. All of the other vegetables were in large tarnished pots; Richard couldn't distinguish the types, all soft and green with pieces of pork skin and fat immersed in the thick green mush. Someone had brushed hot barbecue sauce over ribs – the thick, brown-red meat was piled high on a silver foil tray. There was a turkey with brown wrinkled skin, the fat still bubbling around it, and seven plates of corn bread. Richard's rows of potato skins stuffed with themselves and topped with bacon stood out as starkly as the five white faces that dotted the room.

One whole table was set up for desserts; he could practically smell the sugar. He knew there were secret ingredients in the pecan pie, the mysterious thick brown filling, the nuts and butter and brown sugar. He knew he had to wait for the blessing, but he hoped they would hurry up with it.

Pearl's supervisor, a black woman in a tight, sky-blue rayon dress, clanked the pitcher of thick sweet iced tea with a glass.

"Mr. Rowe will lead us in prayer."

Richard was confused – Mr. Rowe? Mr. Rowe who sat in the corner, rhyming man with can with ban?

Mr. Rowe stepped forward, dignified.

"We will all join hands in a circle."

Everyone shuffled around the circle; it took a few minutes for the noise to quiet down. Richard was between Pamela and Pearl. He bowed his head like everyone else.

"Dear Lord,"

Before Mr. Rowe finished his sentence, several people shouted, really shouted, "Yes, Lord."

"We thank you for the Thanksgiving..."

"Yes, Lord."

"And our ability to work...."

"Yes, Lord."

The "Yes, Lords" seemed arbitrary – Richard could not anticipate when one would come.

Mr. Rowe's voice rose, as if he knew that Richard was thinking of something else, not concentrating on the group.

"All of the labor of man is for his naught and yet the appetite is not filled. For what hath the wise man more than the fool?"

"Is he reading?" Richard asked himself. He felt like a naughty boy, lifting his head and opening his eyes, but he had to look at Mr. Rowe. Mr. Rowe wasn't reading — he knew the passages by heart. He looked right at Richard, breathed in deep, pausing for his own next round.

"We are here to give thanks. Not murmur or mutter thanks. But give it. This is an EXHORTATION to praise..."

Richard snapped his head back down, shut his eyes tight.

"An Exhortation to Thanksgiving. A Psalm of Praise. Make a joyful noise unto the Lord, all ye lands. And that means *all* ye lands. Enter into His gates with Thanksgiving, and into His courts with praise."

"Yes, Lord," Richard said barely audible, feeling hypnotized.

Mr. Rowe's voice was getting softer, "And please remember Mr. Richard, our teacher who teaches us so good. If he can't learn you, nobody can."

And then there was a chorus of "Yes, Lords" from his class.

He felt his face get warm knowing that he must be bright red, even his ears. He sweated, under his arms and on his palms, and squeezed the hands that held his. And for the first time with this group, he was not thinking of their reactions and his response, he was only aware of his body.

Richard let Pearl pile his plate with ribs and corn bread and watched nervously as she added an overflowing scoop of stewed lima beans. He was surprised by the reverence with which the group served each other from the buffet tables, their quiet, rather than exuberant joy. They sat in a large circle around the edges of the waiting room with plates on their laps. Richard crumbled the corn bread with his fingers, savored the fatty juice of the ribs it soaked up. The corn bread was grainy and the ribs were moist. He ate until he was weighed down. When finally he was allowed to eat the pecan pie, he was startled; it was so sweet, it was bitter.

The mountains of food dwindled and Pearl's supervisor once again clanged the sweet tea pitcher with her glass. The shrill signal sounded distant to Richard, but the people who surrounded him were suddenly active. They began working as a team to clean up the party. Richard watched, his plate soggy on his lap. Pearl and the other women gathered the crumbs and the napkins, filling green-black trash bags while others carried away the plates and tureens. Meanwhile, the men started the vacuum cleaners, so that the waiting room vibrated like trucks on the highway. Pamela and Pearl lifted the white tablecloths straight up from the tables. Each stood at one end grasping the corners, then they walked toward each other, folding the cloths in halves in a stylized dance. The men folded the tables and chairs and stacked them on a long dolly. Edna handed Richard his potato tray, washed and dried, wrapped in plastic. Richard had never seen a party get cleaned up so fast.

He tried to breathe in the smells of the meats, the fatback, and the piercing sweet sugars, deeply again and again, but he could only feel the asbestos dust falling, softly like ash into his lungs.

Cross-Over

I had this daydream in French class that I kept it, and brought it into school one day like Mary's little lamb. I had that picture of me in taffeta, dressed up like those girls in the paper for the debutante ball. The nurse told me to think of something pretty, and that's the image I hung onto until the fourth stick in my cervix. And then I started crying. They shoot in four needles and it hurts so bad you want to vomit. The nurse held my hand real tight, like she was going to break it, and I squeezed it back, but I was crying and gagging. She kept telling me that it would pinch a little. Pinch, hell, it felt like somebody had just fired a gun in there.

I'd lost my confidence waiting outside the clinic. I think I might have been able to get through without crying if I hadn't had to wait so long in the rain. It had been my luck to get an abortion the same day that all these people decided to block the doors to the clinic, and I couldn't get inside. So I had to wait. I was with my mom, but I felt like I was all alone. I mean, she was pretty cool to be there and everything, but I kept thinking about Kevin, and thinking he was beside me too. But he didn't want to come. "I know I'm being a sonofabitch," he'd said, which made me forgive him.

The people that were blocking the doors were singing a song that kept repeating itself, "Jesus is coming soon, morning night or noon." Most of the Jesus people were sitting down in front of the double glass doors on top of folded newspapers. One woman who wasn't used to sitting on the ground kept getting pushed around, and you could see her underpants – the white balloon kind that you stop wearing in the fifth grade. A few of the Jesus people kept circling me like flies. "Don't do it honey," one of them said to me. "Your baby could have beautiful thick black hair just like yours." My mom kind of grabbed my elbow, because she knows I like to answer back.

I don't know what I would have said anyway. I was real hungry 'cause they don't let you eat anything before you go in, so I don't think I could have thought up anything smart anyway.

Finally, these two nurses from the clinic came outside. They were wearing these identical blue scrub shirts, like pajama tops, and their hands were soft and smelled like band-aids. I love that smell. "You don't have to wait out here," one of them said. "You could reschedule."

"Oh hell," I said, and I looked over at my mom. "I don't want to have to come back. Anyway, I can't go without food again. I just want to get it done."

My mom kept her hand on my elbow and kept looking over at the door.

"Jennifer, honey, she's right," she said. "You don't have to prove anything today."

"Just stop it. I want to do this, damnit." God, you'd think I could get through one day without yelling at my mom, but the nurses just ignored it, and actually, she did too.

Finally, the younger one said, "We'll wait with you then; let's move over to the corner."

So we set out for the corner which was only like twenty yards away, but we were walking like a giant dust ball. I mean, here are me and my mom, and then these two nurses who opened their umbrellas behind them, and then a few of the Jesus people circled us, yelling things at me. And then all of the sudden I got this flash that we look like a giant womb. That I'm really the fetus, and these women in blue shirts are like all that goop around it.

The Jesus woman said, "Just let us talk to you." And then real sweet, "Are you afraid to talk to us?" But behind her there was this Jesus man, and he was holding up a sign that had a picture of a bloody baby on it. He just held it up for a long time, and wouldn't look at me. I know enough biology to know that what I was carrying didn't look a thing like his poster.

I sat down on the curb without warning anybody, and the group almost collapsed. I would have laughed, but I was getting colder and hungrier, so I smoked a cigarette. I figured that since I was having an abortion, it wouldn't matter anyway. Since the Jesus people wouldn't let us in the building, I needed to do something while I waited. I wanted to just transport myself back to how it happened; sometimes thinking about it can warm you up. I'm good at blocking out everything around me. I do it all the time in French class especially. I know how to tune out the verbs and think about Kevin — a lot of the time it's just the idea of Kevin.

My sister Carla told me not to start so early. She said that once you start you just can't stop after that. I guess she was right. But that was about all she'd say – I learned all the other stuff on my own. And all the time, I'm real careful. You know, because I carry condoms in my backpack.

Behind me on the doorsteps there was a Jesus girl that was my age. She had on a pair of torn up blue jeans, and her hair was pulled

back, and she looked excited. They were singing these hymns that all
sounded like Christmas carols. In a way they sounded kind of pretty
– almost like I could join in just to keep warm.

It was kind of tempting, but all I really wanted to think about was
how this happened. Kevin was teaching me how to ski. We'd skipped
school, and Kevin and his best friend Rick and I went skiing, only I'd
never gone before. They promised me that it was pretty easy. But
you know how guys like that are. Kevin took me on this short cut; I
guess he thought it would be funny. And the next thing I know I'm
tumbling down the slope into the trees, and Kev's trying to keep up
after me, only he's not as good as he thinks he is. He can't keep up,
and so finally he falls too, and slides right into me, and we hit this
tree. My skis have fallen off by this point, and we're laughing so hard
that it doesn't matter. We ended up in a clump of trees. I was ready
to go down the rest of the trail on my butt, but Kevin grabbed me,
and he buried his face in my back, and pulled me up by the back of
my waist. I'm leaning against this tree – the sun's out and we can
see over to the next mountain. He whispered in my ear, "I love your
butt." I don't care – it makes me feel warm to hear a line like that. He
leaned me against the tree and rubbed his hands up and down my
back inside my jacket. I reached behind me and unzipped his pants,
and then he reached around the front and unzipped my ski pants,
and he pressed behind me so I wouldn't get cold. And we did it there
in the woods on that mountain. I don't know, I thought real briefly
about not having any condoms with us, but who would think to bring
them on the chair lift? They were in my backpack, safe, down in the
cafeteria. Well, that was how I got pregnant, I knew it then somehow,
and I wasn't surprised when I missed my period. I don't know – I
mean, I was mad at myself, and nervous — a baby is the last thing you
need when you're in the tenth grade. I want to graduate high school
early 'cause I hate it. So, I don't know.

I stared out at my view of the umbrellas the women from the clinic
held out like shields around us. I could see them cringing from my
cigarette smoke.

"Awful weather," one of them said.

She was only wearing her cotton scrub shirt, so I knew she must
have been freezing.

"Yeah, but it means more snow in the mountains for skiing," I said.

"Skiing's great," she said.

"My boyfriend is going to teach me how."

I saw my mom flinch. She didn't know how it happened, and she
knew she couldn't forbid me from seeing Kevin, but she told me last

night I had no pride when I said I was going to continue seeing him. I mean, he admitted he's being a sonofabitch. Kevin promised to teach me how to ski for real next time. So I repeated it: "He'll teach me when it's good spring skiing...not too many crowds."

"Don't let him take you on anything too rough," the younger nurse said.

That reminded me of Carla and her advice about Kev: "Don't let him talk you into anything." Not that he did.

"Skiing's just like sliding," the younger nurse was saying. "You just get used to it. Gravity and umm..." She looked over at the poster of the bloody baby. "Gravity – how to pull your weight over."

"I know how to water ski," I said.

"There you go," the younger one spoke again. "If you know that, you won't have any problem."

"No, there's not much similar in the two." This is the first I've heard the older nurse speak. "The two sports are nothing alike."

"Yes they are," the younger one said. "I've done both."

"There is no cross-over."

And the next thing I knew, it felt like they're going at it like a couple little kids. You know: is too/is not.

I managed to block them out, too. Skiing will be just like screwing Kevin. I know it.

The police started carting off the people that were blocking the doors to the clinic. This one man, he'd gone limp; he must have weighed two hundred pounds. The police grunted like they were carrying a live cow, and kind of mashed him into the police car. And then the rest of the Jesus people, they started singing even louder. "Rejoice, Rejoice...."

My mom looked over at them. "I wish we could change the channel," she said, biting her grin. Sometimes I really love her.

When the police grabbed the girl that was my age, she started screaming. Her hair had come undone, and the plastic handcuffs dug into her wrists. For a second, I looked at her face; she looked real scared, and I felt kind of sorry for her.

I put out my cigarette, and then the younger nurse looked over at the window and nodded. She didn't say anything, but started walking, so we followed her to another office that had a back door. We went fast, so that the Jesus people didn't have time to block our path.

Suddenly, I was inside. And they were still outside. My mom collapsed into a chair, but I didn't want to sit down on that vinyl stuff since I was kind of wet from the rain. You wouldn't think it, but it's only after something like that happens, you start getting kind of shaky. Finally I just kind of sank down.

I picked up a magazine, and I felt like I was in any doctor's office, except that I was shaking. In a way, I could have waited out there all day, just kind of putting it off, like when you're riding in a car and you don't really want the ride to end. That was how I felt when I went skiing with Kevin that time. I wanted to stay in the car, and ride and ride, and feel like we weren't really going to get out and freeze. I wanted to stay in the front seat like I was, turned sideways so I could talk to Rick and Kevin at the same time, and pass back the bottle of Wild Turkey. I kind of dreaded getting out of the car.

Ellen's Red Hawk

Ice reminds Ellen of Red Hawk. She sees him motionless, embedded in ice and crystallized barbed wire. Hot ice. His hand on her thigh. Ellen can reduce her life to what is cold and what is warm. And now she is warm, tucked inside her duplex, surrounded by dust and mold and things to sell on his behalf.

Red Hawk has been in prison three years now. And yard sales full of dusty shoes and cracked teapots won't get him out. But Ellen holds a yard sale for him with each change in season, another superstition like lifting her feet whenever she drives over a railroad track. There's no guarantee that lifting her feet will keep her lover, but she knows the rule that if she doesn't lift her feet, she'll lose her lover. Ellen's lover was Red Hawk. Of course, that's not his name – only what he accused Ellen, the only white woman among Paul Turner's loves, of calling him in her mind.

"Paul." She imagines, propelling her thoughts over the barbed wire, through the cement walls. "I hope you appreciate this." Sometimes Ellen can see an image of him in prison, and sometimes he blurs into the newsprint of the articles she wrote about him. The longer he is in prison, the vaguer his image becomes in her mind.

Ellen holds a cloudy bowl up to the light; she flicks it with her finger and listens to the magically sustained reverberation.

"Real," she says out loud, and prices it accordingly.

Before she left the reservation, there had been a silent solidarity among the women in Paul Turner's life. The talk at the well was bitter: "Framed for a white murder." The women spoke sharply, the frozen air cutting short their words. And the gossip around the tables, laden with coffee and fry bread, was full of strategy. More people joined their circle, though, and that made Ellen cross. The new people sat around creating earnest plans that fell by the wayside when they got their first real jobs. It reminded her of college where the men sat around eating bologna sandwiches and smoking cigarettes, discussing their strategies for marches and boycotts. Only now the stakes seemed higher to her, the strategies just as weak, and her patience thinner. When the summer ended, and she felt the first bitter wind of fall, no one chided her for packing up her little blue truck and heading back south.

On the way home, Ellen visited Paul Turner in prison. The prison smelled like her grade school when someone had vomited and the janitor threw green disinfectant on top of it. She sat in a booth and through three layers of glass she could see him, though the way the glass refracted the light made him look several blocks away. They talked to each other through telephones, and she could see his lips move, but the voice took a second or two to come through the phone. She had traveled two days to talk on the phone to him.

"How are you...?"

It was impossible to tell over the static. Paul smiled more than she did, and the loneliness hardened around her.

When Ellen had first arrived in South Dakota it was to a brown and sooty summer. She came with a tape recorder and some notebooks, ready to cover the aftershocks of Wounded Knee for her small weekly newspaper. There were times over the summer, with so many people descending on the reservation, Indians and non-Indians, that Ellen felt it was a party she couldn't leave.

But after she sent her first two dispatches, her paper ran out of money and stopped paying her. So Ellen went to work on the broken printing press on the reservation. She churned out greasy copy for the reservation's newsletter, and before she knew it, summer had left, replaced by a browner fall. As the weather cooled off, the crowds dwindled.

"She won't make it through the winter," Ellen heard Min say by the well. Already, when the women gathered at the well in the morning to drag their water home, smoke formed around their words in the air.

"She's no bigger than a minute."

"There's less of me to keep warm," Ellen said as she took her place in the circle, dipping her bucket deep into the well, feeling her forearms burn even before she lifted.

In the early evenings, she sat with the women in their kitchens and gossiped and chopped along with them, around messy tables layered with flour, carrot peels, and potato skins. In the center was the big plate of fry bread – lumpy, sweet clumps of fried dough. They reached across for pieces, not minding their arms getting dusted with flour and juice. Everything went into the dented aluminum stew pot: potatoes, meat, water, beer.

"Do you measure each slice, Ellen?" Gayle laughed. "Look, just let the knife fly."

"Feel how you cook – it isn't science class," Min added.

Ellen was stubborn, though, and continued to slice neat rounds of carrots, perfectly julienned zucchini, about a quarter as much as any other woman chopped.

"Look," she'd say. "Perfect."

"Ha," Gayle said.

Maybe she would have moved on, after she'd proved to herself that she wasn't like the other summer hangers-on. But she'd proved herself too well, and that spring, Ellen got the chance to drive Paul Turner to Colorado.

He had been invited to speak, as usual, this time at a conference on Native American land restitution at a surprisingly conservative college. Ellen was sent along to pass out the leaflets she'd been printing. Turner had been the subject of a few nights of gossip, and Ellen wondered what was going to be true, and what parts of him she'd embellished in her mind. She let them load milk crates full of her reservation newsletters in the bed of her dented blue truck, and then he filled the cab with tales. Ellen listened to the cadence of his speech as it carried over the long stretch of the flat highway, and out of the corner of her eye she watched his hands accompany his words. Huge, articulate hands – they could reach an octave and a half.

His voice was deep and curled; he practically sang his stories, so that Ellen could not have repeated any of them – could only repeat their essence – a playful trick, a bad break, revenge-sweetened justice.

When they reached Colorado and the road got steeper, Ellen broke in.

"Let's be late," she said and smiled. "I know a great trail. It's steep and grown over in places and brambly, but at the top there's a falls."

"I figured you for a hiker."

"Of course. I grew up near the Blue Ridge Parkway. We used to go to the mountains all the time."

"I used to walk miles beyond the reservation lines – up in the hills, nobody ever there."

"So you're game?"

"Sure."

The approach to the trail wound its way through a hot open meadow at the edge of the road. From the truck, it looked like a short distance, but as they started walking, the path seemed to stretch, so that the mountain remained distant. The path was overgrown, and the long grasses scratched their calves.

Where the approach finally ended, and the real trail up the mountain began, the air became cool and moist. The trail switched back under the canopy of thick trees. Shafts of light lay across the trail where the high branches let some sunlight through. Hiking with Paul Turner was like hiking with the southern boys she'd grown up with. He pulled back brambles to let her through the tangled parts of the trail, and held out his hand to help her over streams where the stepping stones were too far apart for her short legs.

When they finally emerged above the tree line, the brightness startled them. From the ridge above the trees, they both stopped to look across the valley at the range of mountains in the distance.

"We could almost expect the cavalry up here," Paul said and grinned.

"As the posse lines up across that ridge to save me."

"I bet that when you were growing up, you watched *Gunsmoke* every week. You curled up in front of the TV on a pillow and knew those people like you knew your own family."

"No." Ellen laughed.

"And you pined away for the Virginian."

"Actually, I pined away for Red Hawk."

Suddenly the sky went dark, and the thunder and lightning gave them only a brief warning. The hailstones fell quickly and turned the landscape white. They ran back down the trail and huddled under a tree, taking turns shielding the other from the assault of ice.

"Bullets from heaven," Paul said. Ellen found that his giving them a name lessened their sting.

Just as she began to feel safe again, lightning hit the mountain across the valley, spreading from peak to base like a giant fissure.

"The Hand of God," he said and pointed to the length of the lightning. Paul's comfort made Ellen feel as though she were taking part in a natural ritual. But even so, she didn't share his ease.

"The Hand of Who?" she asked.

"God." Paul said.

"You say it so simply. As if you really believe it."

"I do."

"I don't." Ellen looked away from Paul. "And I find all those people who come to the reservation looking for their spiritual guidance just draining." Ellen felt that she shouldn't speak of this, but the storm made her reckless.

"Ah, well. Them." Paul smiled. "But there's a difference between disdain and belief. They don't keep me from believing, but I don't have to lead them."

"Right."

"Just because someone might trivialize what I believe in doesn't make it any less true."

"But just because you believe doesn't mean I have to."

"Then how do you explain the llama?" Paul was on the verge of laughing.

There above them, picking its way down the trail, was a shaggy brown llama. It was large, overbearing and muddy, yet for some reason, neither of them felt surprised. Ellen felt that she should have been: llamas weren't indigenous. Later, Ellen would read about llama farms and llama tours nearby. Had she had the opportunity, she would have confronted Paul with that simple bit of information. But at that moment, the llama blocked their path and demanded to be acknowledged.

"Look," Paul whispered.

Paul's fingertip outlined the animal in the air.

Just as the llama reached them, the sun burst out, and the hail stopped. It seemed to Ellen that when the hail finally quit, it did so just as abruptly as it began.

She looked into the llama's eyes as it went down the hail-strewn path, taking up the entire width. Paul reached his hand out over the llama's head, and rested it between the animal's ears. Ellen felt giddy as they hiked back down. The sun was too warm, raising wisps of vapor from the wet rocks and off their clothes.

"Paul, why don't we skip this conference? Maybe we could stay somewhere nice in these hills."

He smiled. "Nice idea. But no. This is too important."

"Why? One more talk, a few more leaflets. Maybe a few more signatures. I hate explaining all this so much. Nobody ever understands anyway."

"Maybe not."

"Oh come on. I just mean...."

"I know. I just can't miss this. People will forget about us. It'll just be a fad unless we keep going."

Ellen shrugged. "Maybe not."

"I can't be a fad," he said, facing her. "Not someone else's image of Red Hawks and Running Bears."

When they finally arrived that night, their hosts from the college showed them their basement guest room. Since it was late, they couldn't tell that there was no window behind the curtains on the wall, but the depths of the room still chilled them. The curtains themselves had a faded print of fish and crosses.

"See?" said Ellen. "That's why I can't take any spirit seriously."

"You make it sound like it's a weight."

"It is, when you grow up with it on billboards and even curtains."

On a mattress in the middle of the cement floor, Paul Turner held Ellen and told her a story about the power of sunlight and the steam it can induce, about a llama that could herald the dawn, and the power of the Hand of God. He held her for a long time before he eased her shoulders flat against the mattress and kissed her neck. "Red Hawk," she whispered to him, and finally he laughed. As they made love in the cold basement, Ellen thought she smelled the Colorado pines around her. She felt warm there until she heard the clank of the pots and pans above them in the morning. They didn't discuss religion again. Shortly after they got back, Paul was arrested, and they never had another chance.

Ellen's happy when people arrive to evaluate her yard sale. No guards or conversations shrouded in mist. No images traded up over razor wire and through concrete walls. Some of the buyers are the same people who donated items in the first place. They support each other's causes by buying these same pieces and donating them again, circulating their small bills and blocks of time. At the end of the day, what she doesn't sell will go to the Environmental League Holiday Bazaar, the South African Solidarity auction.

Ellen tries to keep an eye on people, offers to lower prices, barter, throw in extra pieces. It's like a game to her.

"If you take the basket, I'll throw in the plant. The goldfish bowl with the recorder. A mango with the banjo."

She's good and she sells a lot for Paul's defense fund. Maybe enough for xeroxing and postage, or a token fee to one of the lawyers. It doesn't seem like he even knows about this bargaining for justice. Swap 'n' Shop for freedom. She imagines the monotony of Paul's life now. And she wonders if she's made her life mirror his while she plays games with small change. She goes inside to tuck away some of the money.

"So Ellen," her friend Susan from the Environmental League says, following her inside. "What's new on the Turner case? You're in touch with him directly aren't you?"

"It's been a dead wire," she admits. "No word of any kind." She's embarrassed by the lack of contact from Paul. She doesn't usually state it so bluntly. It can't help her cause. She wishes that Susan would rejoin the crowd on the yard. But Susan is persistent.

"He's a spiritual soul, isn't he?" Susan blocks the door. "That's what I've read about him, anyway."

"It's hard to explain," says Ellen. "It's not typical. You can't quantify it."

Ellen is quiet, and Susan takes the hint and goes back outside.

As she opens the porch door, an unseasonably cool fall breeze comes in. The cold wind hits Ellen, and still she doesn't move from her doorway.

She can hear the group in her yard, drumming their fingers on the plates and glasses, clicking the knobs on the radio she marked "broken," pawing through the boxes of sweaters like mice. She stands with her back to them for a long time, not knowing what she is looking for.

She wishes she could believe in llamas. A llama that could block her path again, demand her attention. She could climb on its back and they would pick their way down her steps, past the broken toasters and chump change. Her bare feet would grip the llama's wiry fur, as the Hand of God rested lightly on her shoulder.

The Possum Ride

Centrifugal force was the only concept she learned well in high school, and she has put it to good use her whole life. Centrifugal force has even kept her employed until now. So it's with some regret that she finds the only jobs available to her require centripetal force instead: receptionist or cashier. At least that's what she imagines those jobs require. Middle-of-the-road jobs that worship their own gravity.

Jenny Majors has prepared for the interview despite her reservations: hair, make-up, stockings — the works. She's practiced introducing herself and mimed shaking hands. She unbolts her door and forces it open. Just as she steps onto her front porch, she sees the possum. It makes eye contact with her, its long grey nose serving as an exclamation point, before it rears up on its hind legs and hisses, baring its teeth. She runs back inside and slams the door. She knows about possums: their ugliness is exceeded only by their viciousness. She lifts a corner of the window shade and stares outside.

Dead possums are on her back porch. Dying possums are on her windowsills. She racks her brain for authorities she can call. Animal Control told her to call Wildlife and Wildlife told her to call Animal Control. Jenny Majors is spending the day on the phone staring at the dying and the dead. She counts three baby possums, and two mothers prowling around them. The mothers hiss at Jenny through the glass. She thinks they must be rabid. The babies are, certainly. They drag their hind legs. Froth at the mouth. The mothers, she's not so sure about. They seem intent on protecting the twitching, long-tailed children, by circling her house and rearing up as they pass her windows. What made them decide to descend on her little house? She debates the possibility of outrunning them, but the mothers seem so athletic with their massive gray bodies. Besides, she's all dressed up. Well, for her. White pressed blouse and even a skirt. The shoes are wrong, but that won't matter if she can't leave the house.

She waits for Animal Control and Wildlife. And her job interview window closes. She could call Human Resources, but what would she say? "I can't be your receptionist. I'm imprisoned by possums."

Jenny has never been jobless before. Even in the winter, when Lost Wonderland was closed for the season, she could get by on odd jobs there, repairing the tracks or repainting the cowboys. She misses more than just the routine, now that she can't go back. She misses the crowds that shoved each other on the sticky, asphalt paths; she misses the staccato organ music that blared from speakers nailed to the trees. She even misses Bill sometimes, with his black jeans and emphasis on fun.

Fun. That was all that was supposed to matter. A microcosm of America, where everyone asked, "Did you have fun?"

"But if it's supposed to be so much fun, why did you name it Lost Wonderland?" Jenny often asked Bill when he flew in to check on his park. "That makes it sound unsettling."

"People like to be disturbed. Just a little – you know, without real risk."

Jenny understood. She liked walking the dusty paths at Lost Wonderland, but she had been careful to learn the layout early on. The three sections – rides, games, water park — were laid out in a circle. If you followed the path, you would go seamlessly from one section to the next. There was not a way to get lost. But people did. Every day Jenny saw them wandering, hot and sunburned.

She saw them try to get their bearings using the wooden cowboy cutouts, but cowboys dotted every path. The people circled the park, stopping to photograph their children, until they were all hungry for the hot dogs and French fries and fried dough stands that littered the trails.

"It's like you're spinning them blindfolded," Jenny told Bill.

"No, it's like running in a cornfield maze. You get lost, so you get scared. It's all part of the fun."

"Loss doesn't scare me," Jenny said. She busied herself with the buttons on his shirt, so he was too distracted to respond. She didn't want him to.

Jenny is used to loss.

All along, she's purposely lost all but the essentials, starting with her name: Jenny Jenkins. One of the many mistakes her mother made. Jenny Jenkins. Almost as bad as Robert Roberts or John Johnson. "It's the same name twice," Jenny told the judge when she changed her name legally.

"The same name twice." Or even worse, where she was from, the Jenkins was pronounced Jinkens, which grated on her ears, making her name sound like a jinx.

If only the rest of the reinvention were as easy as the name. She chose Majors, because it sounded both strong and whimsical, like a military marching band. And then she chose Lost Wonderland, for many of the same reasons.

Bill himself taught her how to operate the rides. She was already Jenny Majors, and he was already married. It didn't matter to her. The other women frowned at her. But that really didn't matter to her either. First came the Lost Can-Can Teacups, then the Pirates' Shipwreck. Sex came after hours behind the water park lagoon. There's an advantage to reinventing yourself. And there's an advantage to being hidden and even to being alone. And that's what Jenny banked on.

Hiding was easy, as were the Teacups. She could make them swoop around the track with her eyes shut. The people inside the cups could make them spin as they were propelled backward. It didn't look fun to Jenny, but it was the ultimate centrifugal force. And that she understood.

When Bill wasn't in town, Jenny smoked cigarettes with the other drivers. They'd meet up, all sweaty by the time the park closed, underneath Joe's roller coaster, the Crazy Lost Kitten. They'd lean against the supports and gossip while they smoked.

"Why do you hang out with Bill?" Joe asked her.

"He keeps me off-balance. Lost, like we're supposed to be." Jenny was able to say it with a straight face, so that Joe continued to question her.

"Why would you want that?"

"She's fucking with you," Benjy knocked Joe's shoulder. "You know not to ask her about Bill. She won't tell you anything. We've all tried."

Jenny smiled. "No, I'll tell you about Bill."

Benjy just shook his head, but Joe leaned forward.

"It's all for fun. That's more important than anything. He's obsessed with it."

"As if we're having fun," said Benjy.

"Not us," said Jenny. "We don't really matter to him that much."

"Then I don't get why you'd stay with him," said Joe.

"It's the idea that there's a place that's designed only for fun. I like that he's so fanatical —"

"You mean rabid," said Benjy.

Joe snorted, and Jenny smiled along with them. "Maybe," said Jenny. "But I like that idea too. I like that people can scream for joy."

"I like the paycheck," said Benjy.

When Bill was away, Joe took to coming over to her little house that overflowed with stuffed bears and gilded fish.

"Where do you get all this stuff?"

"I win it."

"I can't believe you win all the time. I thought the games were stacked against you."

"They are, but I've learned how to defy gravity."

She rarely lost at the Wild West Shooting Range. "Don't aim at the X," the guys working the games told her. She didn't. She aimed where her high school physics told her to. And she won her plush, life-sized dogs and American flag bunting on her own.

Jenny poured their drinks into her circus mugs. She loved the way the handles were formed from elephant trunks and giraffe necks. She'd worked hard to win the whole set. She set out fresh fruit on the matching carnival plates.

"Here. You can't get apples in the park."

"I know. How can you stand it?"

"What?"

"The smell of fried food."

"You are in the wrong business, Joe."

"I know. But I don't know much else. Why do you stay? I know you won't talk about him, but it isn't because of Bill."

"No." For once, Jenny tested the idea of being sincere. "I feel like I can just stay in one place for a while until I figure out what I need to add to my life."

Joe laughed. "If I didn't know better, I'd say you were being honest for once."

Jenny pulled Joe to the back of her house. "Here. Let's shower first. We're both too sweaty."

It was a relief to shower, and even more of a relief to have sex. In the morning, Jenny feigned sleep while Joe put his damp clothes back on and slipped out.

Jenny knew that Joe felt bad for leaving quietly. But she preferred it to apologies or pleas for discretion. She had no need to be encumbered. She was supposed to want more than Bill. She was supposed to want more than her little rented house full of kitschy humor. She was supposed to strive.

And yet she couldn't. She was stuck, but she wasn't worried, even though she knew she should be. The truth was that she didn't let much bother her. Not the heat, not the crowds, not the noise. Sometimes the water park bothered her, with its curving tubes that discharged people into vats of gray water. And sometimes, if she wanted to feel something, she might call her mother. Then she knew she could still feel pain. And that would reassure her.

Because with reinvention comes loss. And even when the loss is called for, it's still loss.

Her home had been broken. That's how she'd originally heard her friends' mothers describe it. They didn't know how accurate they were. But those parts were secret. Once she tried to tell her best friend, Kaitlin Pettit, some parts – her mother's temper, the bruises on the backs her legs – but Kaitlin, with her Waspy, balanced name just looked at her.

So she calls her mother and learns that she could be so pretty if she only let her hair grow out. She learns that Kaitlin is majoring in business. And she learns again that her mother doesn't believe in the gospel truth.

Eventually, Bill promoted her, and she learned the Lost Sailor Roller Coaster. It wasn't shiny or fast like Joe's Crazy Lost Kitten, but it would do. Perpetually sunburned, hair short and spiked, she still caught herself smiling when she heard the crowds scream. They sounded delighted, almost hopeful.

The Lost Sailor was plain and fairly slow. The one nautical theme among the dry rides, it revolved on a metal track high above the park. At the top, before the dip, you could see the water park. From the peak, you could wave to the folks on the Lost Ness Monster Log Flume. Jenny didn't like the way she was supposed to make the Lost Sailor stop there at the peak – just briefly to let the riders see the beauty of Lost Wonderland.

"But Bill," she said, as he taught her the controls. "It's not beautiful."

"It could be. If you don't stop the ride for too long, people will think it's beautiful."

"Just because you have a vista doesn't mean you have beauty."

"Are you sure?" Bill wrapped his arms around her. He'd gained some weight, which didn't bother her either. It wasn't too much, and he was still obsessed with amusement.

So she let it go, and she operated the Lost Sailor. Sometimes she would test it out, when Joe could drive it in her place. From the top, so briefly, she could see the organized chaos on the paths. Or sometimes she'd concentrate on the trees. They added depth, but not beauty. Sometimes, she concentrated on the water park from the top of the Lost Sailor track. She'd always heard that waterfalls made people happy – the negative ions or something. But she didn't think that fake waterfalls had the same effect. No matter how much she liked Lost Wonderland, she could not call it beautiful.

On the morning that the girl fell out of the sky, Jenny hadn't had a chance to get sweaty yet. She had just started her shift, and the air was remarkably dry and breathable. First the girl was in her Lost Sailor car above the park. Then Jenny stopped the car just for the instant she was supposed to so that the riders could see the beauty of the park. And then the girl was on the ground. The girl didn't seem to have time to scream, but the screams of the other passengers drowned out what should have been the loud whump as the girl hit the pavement. The sound that stays with Jenny is the hiss of breath leaving the girl's lungs. There is an image in Jenny's mind of the girl falling from the sky, but she doesn't know which parts she's imagined and which parts actually happened. She sees one sharp frame with the girl frozen mid-way, her bra strap showing outside her tank top, her shorts perfectly ragged. But Jenny suspects there's no way she could have stopped time that way.

At the top, before the dip, the girl must have seen the water park. She could see the fake waterfall and watch it soak the people on the Lost Ness Monster. And she could wave to them as they screamed from the shock of the splash. Most people on the Lost Sailor just stuck their arms high above their heads. Every so often, teenagers would stand. And every time, until now, they had gotten away with it. So it really wasn't Jenny's fault that the girl fell out. They had proved that in court.

Jenny wanted to quit the day the girl tumbled out of her roller coaster car.

But Bill wouldn't let her quit until the trial was over. "It wouldn't look right," he told her.

Of course, the girl falling out of the sky didn't look right either. Jenny played it over and over in her mind. Always buckling the strap across the girl's waist. Always running the cars at just the right speed. Still, no matter how often she saw the scene, she could never absolve herself. No matter how perfect she had been, the scene always ended with the girl in the sky.

So Jenny went back to operating the Teacups, which were easy, and their centrifugal force, which she understood. The people were never far off the ground, but they screamed anyway. It grated on Jenny now.

"I can't stand the sounds anymore," she told Joe over cigarettes.

"But if you quit, you can't get unemployment," he reminded her. "What would you live on?"

"I'd figure out something. This place makes me feel too exposed."

"You told me when I first met you that you'd already lost everything. You were a clean slate. Just hiding out here."

"I was wrong."

Bill appeared in court in a suit. His wife was in a suit, too, and sat behind him. Jenny put on a skirt and shoes that didn't match. Bill's lawyers told her not to say much, as if she would have. As soon as the jury decided that the girl had stood to wave to her friends on the log flume, Bill let her take her leave.

"If I fire you, you can get unemployment," he told her.

And that was the nicest thing he had ever done for her.

Joe walked her to her car on her last day. "It'll be okay," he told her. "It wasn't your fault." Hearing him say it was better than hearing the jury say it, but it didn't make any difference.

Sometimes Jenny misses the humor of her kitsch, all the toys she'd won shooting the Lost Cowboy's rifle. But she'd stashed the bunting and the flying pigs and the fuzzy monkeys into black trash bags and dropped them off at Goodwill the day after she was fired. Her little house is barren now, which is good, because maybe Animal Control or Wildlife will take her seriously whenever they show up.

She watches the possums through her window. "If I ever talk to him again, I should tell Bill to create the Lost Possum Coaster," she thinks. Where terror meets fun.

Jenny slices an apple and washes off her make-up. She didn't want to be a receptionist anyway. Who would she receive and how? But what's next? Of course, nothing's next until the possums leave. And they just won't.

In the morning, the possums are gone. Maybe Animal Control came by while she was sleeping. Or maybe Wildlife came by while she was dreaming of the converse elements of gravity. That is the dream she usually has. That the girl bounces back into her car. Or the girl floats in the sky. Or that Bill had sprung for a net. Sometimes she dreams that she has time to fix the girl's bra strap. She racks her brain for the physics lessons she's forgotten. There has to be some chapter on weightlessness. Some way to harness that buoyancy. But gravity always wins.

NICU

Becca Steward was sweating underneath her scrubs. The radiant warmers toasted her more than they did the infants. The room was noisy, filled not with the sound of babies crying, but with the sound of machines — the ventilators whirring, and the shrill beeping and buzzing of the monitor alarms. A baby well enough to make a noise didn't belong here.

Becca was aware of the seventeen-year-old hanging back from the crib that held the twins, Baby Rivers A and Baby Rivers B. Two days after the birth of her twins, Angela Rivers still hadn't washed the sweat of delivery out of her hair or named her children.

Under the fluorescent lights, Becca snaked the tubes and wires up to the babies while a nurse kept the leads out of the way of her fingers. Heart monitor, lung monitor, IV flow monitor.

"Shit," she said under her breath: the chest tube had slipped. That one had been the hardest to put in — such a tiny space between the two ribs. As the nurses hurried over to help Becca fix the chest tube, Angela Rivers was pushed closer and closer to the isolette that held her babies.

Angela jerked her head up. "What's wrong? Is he dying?"

Becca shook her head, "Nothing. Just this tube."

She wished she were as calm as she sounded. But the trocar, a solid piece of metal for inserting the chest tube, was huge compared to the baby's chest. As she rammed the thick metal through his chest wall, she felt the nurses watching her hands.

The twins were fetuses really — six months inside Angela Rivers' belly. Ten years ago, or even six, the Rivers Twins would have died, would have been left for dead. And even now, Becca wondered, as much as she felt she ought not wonder, if they would be better off dead than retarded.

If she had seen Angela even a few minutes before she had gone into labor, she might have told her that it would still be legal for her to have a saline abortion. But now she was working hard to help the babies breathe, or at least exchange air.

Baby B's rheumy eyes were open, almost focused. His skin was gelatinous, like congealed fat. Becca stuck her finger into the isolette. She touched the fingertip-sized hand, and Baby Rivers B curled his tiny fingers around her pinky.

The grasping reflex. It reassured her, every time. She had spent some months in the intensive care ward in the veteran's hospital. Every morning she would do the rounds on the men. "Mr. Giovanni," she would have to shout, "MR. GIOVANNI. Can you hear me? If you can hear me, grab my finger." Very slowly, Mr. Giovanni would wrap his fingers around hers. She would try to finish her exam, but soon she would have to shout as kindly as she could, "OK, MR. GIOVANNI, you can let go of my finger now. LET GO OF MY FINGER NOW." And reluctantly, his fingers uncurled from hers.

"Now you try it," she said, and motioned to Angela who stepped forward, shoulders hunched, and pressed her little finger against Baby B's palm. She smiled and shuddered slightly when his fingers closed around hers.

Becca pecked on the computer, leaving Angela leaning over the rim of the isolette, twirling a strand of her blonde hair.

"They should be stable for now," Becca said.

As soon as Becca walked out of the NICU, she pulled off her wet mask, wiped her face with the back of her hand. She stood above an air-conditioning unit trying to dry herself.

Yes endotracheal tube. Yes chest tube. These decisions, calls of judgment seemed arbitrary. In the NICU, it seemed like you just did everything until nothing worked. In her own life, she worked in the same methodical way, trying to keep track of the elaborate set of rules that she and Nate had set up. Yes dinner. Yes late night notes.

Becca sat down in the conference room that overlooked the courtyard, her favorite place to work. She poured herself a cup of throat-scalding coffee and agonized over her charts. Becca looked at the ceiling. She knew she had spent too long with Baby B — just a ghost of Baby A, smaller, weaker. And damn, the chest tube probably wouldn't save him — why subject him to that? She was never able to separate herself from the deaths and the impending deaths. Beginning with her first — old Mr. Giovanni, who had been rotting alive so that they always had to keep a window open — to now, each death was a part of her. There was no separation. She knew that a doctor who became cold or separate shouldn't work until a few nerves became raw again. It was important to stay in that fine gray area between compassion and precision.

Becca sipped the coffee; she liked to drink it hot, almost sterile. She stared out the sliding glass doors onto the patio in the courtyard. The kids on the ward had dotted the doors with messages — "Watch Out!" "Bird Death!" — in an effort to keep the birds from crashing in. Becca had been watching a family of cardinals in the yard. She followed the birds' lives, as if they were part of a soap opera. This was their second year here, and Becca liked to think it was the same family. In the morning, the scene was still. Dianacat, the fat striped cat who was fed by every nurse and every pediatric patient, sprawled on the deck, eyeing the birds. The birds took her for granted. On the far railing of the balcony a squirrel watched the cat, watched the feeder. Becca saw inside the squirrel's mind, round and round. "There's the food, but there's the cat. But the cardinals are eating. And there is the food, but there's the cat."

She was supposed to be deciding whether or not to move out. She would supposedly be on her own. Just for three months, supposedly. She and Nate had set the end of the week as their deadline. If she were to move out, there would be a deadline on that too. That way, no decision would be permanent, no decision fixed. There's the marriage, but there's her lover, but there's the child; and there's the marriage, but there's the lover. Cat. Bird. Squirrel. Food. Babies. Death.

She'd worked in Nate's lab when she had been a resident. He had shown her how to perform the experiments — careful, sterile procedures. Each drop of liquid painstakingly exact. She'd liked the lab. Liked the way Nate's dark hair looked against his white lab coat. He was always surprising her then. A bottle of vodka in the freezer that held the mice. Little notes stuck in between the pages of data. On the other hand, Michael was outside of their sphere. As a travel writer, he wasn't at all concerned with saving lives, but she liked the cheerful way he reported on them. And since he wasn't her husband, she didn't need to count on him to do the dishes or pick up Len from daycare. But Michael didn't seem to understand that that's what made it work.

Last night, after Len had gone to bed, Nate brought in the box from the refrigerator they had just bought. He set the box in the middle of the living room, so that it was impossible not to trip over. Nate had brought the sleepy Len down in the morning and told him it was a new airplane. Len's pudgy fingers patted the side of the box. "You can't find me!" Len shouted, tucked deep inside. "Noodles," Becca said. The code word to say he was found. She'd ruined the moment, she knew. But still she felt a sharp wave of love for them as she sat in the white hospital workroom. And yet, she was restless, too.

"Dr. Steward?" Angela was standing in the doorway. She had tied the sash of her robe so that she wasn't as exposed.

"Come on over, Angela."

Angela sat on the edge of one of the orange, molded plastic chairs. She squeezed her hands over her scalp, then slid them down over her cheeks so that her fingertips rested just under her nose, as if she were praying. She breathed into her hands, "Dr. Steward...are they too young to live?"

"They're not too young to live. They're just too young to be born."

Angela folded her lips together and then smiled. "That's a nice way to put it." She paused and then looked right at Becca.

"You know, at first I wanted an abortion. If they die, it would be kind of like getting one, wouldn't it? Jesus H. Christ. Wouldn't that be weird?"

Becca knew that the question wasn't meant to be answered. She allowed a moment to pass, and then she poured Angela a cup of coffee.

Becca and Angela looked out into the courtyard.

"How much do you expect that cat weighs?"

Becca laughed and said, "Pounds and pounds, and she just keeps growing."

"She's gotta be bigger than both of my babies put together. What's her name?"

"Dianacat. I call her The Fat One."

Angela leaned further back in her chair.

"I wanted to have an abortion at first. I did. But first off, I couldn't afford it..."

"The cost of an abortion," Becca thought and quickly recomposed the letter she'd been meaning to write to someone powerful, "The cost of an abortion is about the same as the cost of an hour in the NICU."

"See, I really couldn't afford it, I mean I had just moved out of my Mom's. Me and Jimmy, we was living in this duplex over behind the mall? It was kind of a dump in ways, but at least it had carpets and drapes and stuff.

"So we was paying a small fortune for our place, and I knew that I was too young and had drunk too much Jim Beam to be carrying no little kid. So it was all set. We were gonna scrape up the money somehow. And then, Jimmy, their Daddy, got on this born again religion kick. He kept saying that this was the way it was meant to be. And that I was carrying God's baby. Can you believe that?"

Angela's hands got busy around her coffee cup and started patting the table. Her voice got tighter.

"God's baby, I mean really." Angela raised her voice. "Finally I just asked him, 'Are we gonna name it Jesus?'"

Becca spurted her coffee. Her laugh came deep from her gut. Angela started laughing too.

For one second they were silent until Angela added, "I mean, is God gonna pay the bills?

"Well you can guess the rest. You ain't seen Jimmy up around here have you?"

Becca shook her head.

"Of course not. Oh, he was fine and cute for a little while, and then he started screwing around. I tell you, I wasn't gonna put up with that shit."

Becca thought, "Funny, those were Nate's exact words. But not mine. I could have made it work."

If Michael, hands like alabaster, hands with hard sinewy muscles and short clipped nails, had not demanded more of her. If Nate had not forced her to choose. She could have made both work, made it all work, if only they would have remained perpetually stable around her. Stability. Flexibility. Michael. Nate.

"...but do you know what bothers me the most?"

Angela leaned toward Becca and lowered her voice.

"It's that they don't look like babies. They look like the baby pigs we had to cut up last year in biology class."

"Oh Angela, they look scary now, but that's normal. I've seen other babies this young turn out very well. Have you seen the pictures?"

Becca felt doctorly and stable as she led Angela over to the bulletin board, and pointed to the pictures of the rounder, pink babies who had once been yellow and full of tubes. Angela studied the photographs for a long time, whispering their names and tracing her finger around the healthy images.

By the time Becca got home, Len was in bed.

Nate was still in the kitchen, stirring dinner for her. From the street she had smelled the sweet tomatoes stewing and too much basil.

Becca tiptoed into Lenny's room. Lenny born pink and fat and healthy. Her first stint in the NICU had coincided with her pregnancy. "Scared the poor baby into staying where he belonged for nine months," Becca used to joke, until the joke got old. Lenny's face was smushed against the pillow. She placed her hand on his cheek and sat on the edge of his bed, staring at him. For a long time, Becca couldn't leave.

In the morning, Becca stopped by Angela's room. She was propped up on the pillows, looking at the TV; unnaturally colored people were on the screen. Deep green faces and pink purple suits.

"How did you make it do that?"

Angela laughed a little. "I thought of some names last night."

Angela looked at the foot of the bed.

"Who am I kidding? I can't afford to keep these babies."

"Shhh. Angela. We'll see. You don't need to make that decision yet. You still have time."

Angela leaned down into the pillows.

Becca's pager went off loud, like a siren. "Excuse me, Angela." Becca ran to the NICU and squinted in the harsh fluorescent light. Two nurses and the respiratory therapist were already gathered around the isolette. Becca listened to the baby, hoping to hear air entry. She turned the ventilator up to ninety breaths per minute, and then watched the needle on the oxygen monitor rise for a moment, then settle back down. If the first procedure didn't work, it was less likely that the second or third would work, but she did them anyway. For more than an hour they worked, prodding, jabbing, and cursing.

"I'll go talk to Angela," Becca said.

Becca sat on the edge of Angela's bed. Her voice, steady and soft, dropped into a lower range whenever she had this conversation.

"I'm sorry. Baby B isn't going to make it. We've tried everything, and even with the ventilator on full blast, we can't get enough oxygen into his blood. If we disconnect him from the respirator, he'll live for a few minutes, maybe an hour or two. If we leave him on it, he'll stay alive for another week or so, maybe until the end of the month. It's hard to predict. Have you thought about what you would want to do knowing this?"

Angela squeezed the blanket between her hands. "Seems obvious to me. Now. Makes sense."

Becca touched Angela's shoulder. "I'll send a nurse to get you in a few minutes."

She began the intricate process of disconnecting the monitor leads and pulling out the tubes. She worked the chest tube out and sewed up the incision. When only the respirator tube was left, she sent for Angela.

Becca pulled out the respirator tube. She carried Baby B over to the corner of the NICU, where Angela sat in a rocking chair behind a screen. From there they could still hear the machines and the footsteps and the monitor alarms. Becca looked at the dark wooden chair where so many women had rocked with their babies, and then handed Baby B to Angela. She left them behind the screen.

When it was time, she walked Angela out to the courtyard, where they sat together like an old couple in a nursing home, watching the animals.

"I'm sorry." Becca couldn't think of anything else to say. Angela cried, but she didn't sob. Like her son, she didn't make a sound.

Going 45

Jill soaked in Tide, even though it left her skin dry, bright white, and puckered like Dotted Swiss fabric. It was a habit, like cocaine, but it was the only way she could get the smells to dissipate. Sometimes, she could go for days without adding Tide to her bath, but then she would cave in, craving the absence of scent, the promise of a fresh start. Jill's jobs permeated her skin, leaving it smelling like fish and sweat, chlorine and the slobber of retarded kids. She had tried designer bath oils, but then she smelled like mahi-mahi or some other fatty fish. She had tried trendy spa scrubs, and while they seemed to help with the fish, they had little impact on saliva and chlorine. Tide was definitely the most effective additive, but it left her prone to infections.

The bathtub was in the kitchen, in one of those apartments that hadn't yet been renovated. The apartment had never been nice. Over the years, the ugly buildings surrounding hers had given way to improvements. Her apartment was still a tenement, which made it almost cheap enough for her to live alone.

Jill soaked in Tide tonight in the clawfoot bathtub next to the refrigerator. Daniel – Daniel Who Wouldn't Leave – perched on the edge. Steam separated his face from hers. She had to keep the water hot, nearly boiling to dissolve the Tide, but she liked the challenge of soaking that way. The heat kept Daniel out of the tub, as well; his face took on a damp sheen, and the red patchy beard that she'd liked so much when she first met him at Molly's Pub, was moist.

"I don't see why you have to add Tide," he said, as he handed her a washcloth. "Have you ever tried lemons?"

"I've tried everything," Jill said, her voice raspy from screaming at her students. "Lemons make me smell like somebody's dinner."

"That doesn't sound so bad." Daniel leaned into the steam to kiss her neck.

"Stop that. I need to soak some more. It takes forever to get clean."

"I bet if you stopped going to Molly's, you wouldn't need the Tide. The alcohol and smoke from out front - that's what you're battling."

"Maybe. But then I wouldn't have met you."

Jill dipped her head back; only her nose and the tips of her breasts pushed up out of the water. She didn't know exactly why she encouraged Daniel. Of course, he was attractive, but that wasn't enough for her usually. Part of it was fear: he had become friendly with her very patient bookie. In fact, that's who had introduced them. So, she felt almost as if she were being watched. But realistically, both of those things could be ignored, and she thought she could get rid of Daniel if she tried just a little harder. On the other hand, she also thought she could get out of debt if she tried a little harder too. Or she could live a simpler life if she tried even harder.

"Gracie went into a seizure and bit me today. Look." Jill pointed to the tiny row of teeth marks on her breast.

Daniel leaned over the tub, steam turning his cheeks pink. "Did you get a tetanus shot?"

"Thank God, I got one last month when I slashed my arm on a grouper. They gave me a tetanus shot when they stitched me up."

"How can you need stitches from a fish?"

"Have you ever seen a grouper's teeth? They're scary. I was delivering the fish, and I didn't want to make two trips, so I had them piled really high. Then, I dropped them, and the next thing I know, I'm bleeding where the teeth ripped through my skin."

"The teeth?"

"I think it was the teeth. I guess it could have been the crate."

"Teeth make a better story."

"Right. Anyway, it was stupid of me. I almost quit that night. But I need the money too much. This apartment…betting on the Yankees…."

"That's all the more reason to come to Toronto with me," said Daniel.

"I just met you. In a bar, yet. Besides, I don't want to go to Toronto. What would I do in Toronto? Rot in some apartment with you? No thanks."

Daniel sighed. "I told you. I have to get back to school. I'll fail if I stay here any longer."

Below them, the street noises grew louder. She tried to ignore the whiny kids, the impatient drivers, all short-tempered from the heat, the sirens, and the car horns, the dog yelps that drifted in through the open window. The sounds disturbed her, but it was too hot to close them out. Jill wanted to think of her apartment as a tiny fortress. She had painted the thin walls white; and except for the Yankees pennant, they were bare.

She pulled the drain on the tub, and the water leaked out slowly. Kneeling in front of the spout, she turned the water back on and rinsed the grains of detergent from her hair. Daniel held out a towel like a curtain, and Jill wrapped herself up, letting her short, brown hair drip onto her shoulders. Daniel was wiry next to Jill. Jill's arms were able to lift the reluctant and the disabled from wheelchair to pool in the daytime, able to carry crates of groupers through service alley entrances at night.

"Come to Toronto – quit your jobs."

"Tell you what. If the Yankees lose, I'll come with you to Toronto."

"Good – "

"But only for a weekend."

"We'll see. You might like it there. You can teach retarded kids to swim there just as easily as you can here. And if you live with me, you won't need to hawk fish. I'll take care of you."

Daniel turned on the radio. "Oh shit," he said. "The game's been rained out. Come here. You are so beautiful."

"No – you have to leave. I told you a week ago — one night. That's it."

"You made a bet. If the Yankees win, I'll go."

Jill let the towel slip down; Daniel put his arms around her and carried her to the bedroom. Jill leaned over and swept the floor with her arm to pick up the whiskey bottle.

In the morning, the apartment was dark and hot. Even with the window open, and the sound of the rain falling past, the air was still inside. Jill and Daniel lay side by side, the sheets crumpled at the foot of the bed.

Jill leaned into the curve of Daniel's neck. She didn't like the feeling when life was calm. She didn't like stopping long enough to think. She didn't like the thoughts that blank morning moments like this afforded.

Jill used to think that the disabled kids she taught lived on a separate plane, that behind their blank stares and thick speech, they were intellectuals on some planet that earthlings couldn't see. But after a couple years of lifting them from wheelchairs, wiping their spit off her shoulder, Jill developed the realism the other classroom teachers shared. After work, they drank together, and Jill won round after round of Name That Student, her arms and legs in wild gyrations. The teachers hated anyone else's discrimination toward their charges – they would defend the kids to the death from an outsider. They could make fun though, because they spent their days there. The prize was beer, and Jill got drunk and bet on the Yankees until she was so far in debt she had to take a second job delivering fish.

When she finally saw Daniel's eyes twitch, Jill yelled, "I'm late! It's all your fault. You have to drive me to work."

"I don't mind," said Daniel. "I'll pick up something for dinner."

"Just not fish."

"Of course not. You need something healthy. I'll surprise you."

They climbed into Daniel's pale green Buick, with its creases and dents. He kept it oddly clean, despite the torn upholstery and scratches on the dash. They were silent on the drive. A quick kiss, and Jill dashed into the Center for Retarded Citizens.

Jill and Teresa lifted Gracie, fat like bread dough, onto the changing bench. Teresa was one of the classroom teachers whose job Jill thought was even more absurd than her own. Teresa taught the activities of daily living. Every day, she taught the students to comb their hair and button their clothes. This, after college and graduate school.

Jill helped Gracie up. "Aren't you going to say hi to the locker room, Gracie?"

"Jill," Teresa hissed. "We're trying to teach her to stop doing that."

But it was too late. "Hi, Locker Room. Hi, Gracie."

Still, they both smiled. Gracie only spoke to inanimate objects.

Together, Jill and Teresa unbuttoned Gracie's blue oxford cloth shirt, unzipped her black jersey skirt, unrolled the socks from her ankles. They helped her squeeze into the industrial black swimsuit. Teresa had never been able to reach Gracie. Gracie drooled on both of them while they patiently undressed and dressed her. They handled her clothes gently, folding them so they fit into the cubby. They handled her lumpy body even more gently; Gracie never acknowledged their touch, but she never hesitated to walk to the pool.

"Hi, Bathing Suit. Hello Gracie." Gracie's eyes seemed to drift apart. She wasn't exactly cross-eyed, but she had trouble staying focused. Jill always wondered if that's why she spoke so much to inanimate objects. Perhaps, unlike people, they stayed still long enough to make a mark.

They escorted Gracie out to the pool, arms on either side to keep her from slipping. Jill eased Gracie into the water and stood behind her, guiding her shoulders backward so that her head pointed up to the ceiling, until Gracie yelled the sound that signaled she was happy. She sounded like a sea gull.

"I'm just like you." Jill said to Gracie. "I scream at Daniel and then I pretend he's inanimate."

"Jill! You were supposed to be getting rid of him."

Jill shrugged. "Maybe it's meant to be. He's going to fix supper tonight."

"Why wouldn't he? He needs a place to stay."

"It's more than that −"

"You're afraid of his friends."

"No, remember? He's patient."

"I know, but I wouldn't push it. That's always seemed precarious to me."

"It is. If I keep my end of the bargain; nothing will happen. I just think with Daniel, maybe it's meant to be."

"I can't believe you. Learn to take your time."

Jill wrapped her arms around Gracie's soft middle. She led her out to the center of the pool so she could splash her arms and pretend to swim in the safety of Jill's embrace. Jill treaded water while she kept Gracie's head up.

Teresa swam over to help bring them back to the ladder. "By the way, we're going to Molly's after work. Join us?"

"Can't. Tonight's a fish night. Besides, you said I have to get rid of Daniel."

"I'm just repeating what you've been saying for the past week. Seriously, though, I'm starting to worry. You live too fast."

"It's okay. He buys the beer. And the whiskey."

"Right. And makes supper. A prince."

Jill grasped Gracie under her armpits. "Here, help me get her out before she seizes again." They lifted her, dripping, back into the locker room.

"Bye, Pool. Bye, Gracie."

"Stop that Gracie. Jesus."

Jill took the blow-dryer and aimed it at Gracie's head. Like an infant, Gracie was helpless, but she smiled as the wind went through her hair. Jill set her dry hair into two long braids. "You look pretty now, Gracie."

Teresa took Gracie's arm. "Say goodbye to Jill."

Gracie looked straight at Jill and said, "Bye, Pool."

The subway ride home was still crowded, even though rush hour had supposedly ended hours before. Jill was smashed between two beefy women and their shopping bags. She could feel the sweat move down her back, making her shirt cling to her skin. Finally, she climbed the stairs to her apartment.

"Hi, Tub. Hi, Jill."

Jill peeled her clothes off and climbed in the bath. Daniel sat on the edge of the tub, watching Jill soak. He'd set the table with Jill's plain white dishes. A vegetable soup simmered on the stove. The smell of cilantro filled the apartment and irritated her. If that were the only thing wrong with the situation. But she knew it wasn't. The gesture was nice, of course. A stranger feeds you healthy soup, but taints it with cilantro.

"Why don't you go back to Toronto without me?" Jill asked, slowly moving the washcloth around her neck.

"Because the Yankees are going to lose."

"They have to win. I can't go to Toronto. Teresa says I live too fast, and that I'll die if I keep this up."

"Teresa doesn't know shit." Daniel said. "She's spent, what, the last five years of her life working with those retards?"

"It's a good job; they need us." Jill said, and dipped her head back into the chalky water. Tide again. She couldn't help herself.

The next night, Jill and Daniel listened to the game on the clock radio – Daniel in his place by the tub, Jill soaking in her white water. When the Yankees lost by one run, Jill felt like the radio had been thrown in the tub with her.

Jill didn't pack much, because she didn't like losing bets. Besides, she had her credit card if she needed a shirt or a toothbrush. The credit card she shouldn't use of course, given her tricky relationship with money, banks, and bookies. But who knew, maybe Daniel really would take care of her there. Just for the weekend. He promised to pay for her flight home if she really wanted to go back. So she told herself that the trip was destined. Losing the bet was destiny. Losing the bet would pay off in the long run. She slid into Daniel's car.

"The Yankees lost, and I'm not talking to you." Jill said.

She might have sulked the whole trip, except that the freedom of the second mile on the road sustained her. Not the first, when the thoughts of picking up mail, and turning off stoves were too present. On that second mile, Jill felt the line that held her to the city gently snap loose.

"Jill, would you hand me a piece of that melon, please?." Daniel asked.

"It needs to soak longer, a melon that size."

In the back seat like a child, a watermelon sat behind a seat belt, soaking up grain alcohol. It had been Daniel's idea, but Jill had gone along with it. When they went to the market to stock up on road food, they bought granola bars, grapes, and the melon. "Only healthy food," Daniel insisted. "You can't drive with a stomach full of greasy sandwiches." Evidently, you could drive with a stomach full of alcohol, because they stopped for liquor as well.

Jill cut a pie-shaped wedge and handed it to Daniel. Bright red melon fruit – thick and sweet. It was a perfect summer melon. Jill cut a wedge for herself. Red juice and alcohol dripped onto her chin as she bit. The cold of the melon against her tongue, against her cheeks eased the hot city smells that drifted in beside her through the open windows. Red, cold melon cut through the heat and the noise, leaving only the hot taste of liquor in her throat.

"Roll up your window, Daniel. We're going into the Lincoln Tunnel."

The thick air inside the tunnel was almost visible. With the windows rolled up, the car was like a box, heat inside and out. Sweat dripped off their faces, onto the gray upholstered seats. The melon seemed to help.

"I didn't think you'd actually come with me."

"I don't break my word. The Yankees lost. Here I am."

By the time they got out of the tunnel, Jill was almost asleep, legs curled up against the dash board, her head on the window, melon rind on the floor.

Dusky, crowded highway stretched ahead; New Jersey smelled like fish and parking lots, and Jill yearned for the feel of an ice cube against her neck. If she could sleep, she could be in Toronto sooner. If she could sleep, she could avoid thinking about the differences between luck and opportunity, between gambling and fortune. She could avoid trying to interpret a horoscope that told her that the moon's position favored a sense of place. So she settled back against the glass, and felt the full weight of the highway.

When the blue light flashed inside the car, Jill had to blink awake. She wasn't expecting to be stopped – only expecting to finish out her part of the bet. But here they were, with a police light flashing in the back seat and the watermelon rind hollowed out like a smashed pumpkin. She heard the policeman's footsteps grow louder behind the car, and when he stuck his face into Daniel's, Jill could have mouthed the words in sync:

"Son, do you realize how fast you were going? Do you know you were going 90?"

How many times had she heard those words – Ma'am, Lady, Son, do you know? – and the responses that varied, tears or apologies or muffled anger. She didn't know Daniel well enough to know his response, but she always thought that those responses told a lot about someone.

"No sir, officer," Daniel said, eyes turned directly to the cop, face straight and stern. "I was not speeding. There are two of us in the car, and we're each going 45."

Jill stifled a laugh, and the policeman stared at Daniel. For an instant, Jill asked herself if he was crazy or only drunk.

"You see," Daniel continued, "Two times 45 is 90." He was so earnest that Jill put her face in her hands and her head on the dash; the policeman opened the car door, and with a large, wise hand tugged Daniel out.

The police station was in the middle of a town that Jill had never seen before; it was hard to make out its shape in the darkness. A western New York town, she guessed. Small, with coffee shops and gas stations and not much else.

Jill waited on the bench in the hallway while they questioned Daniel. She thumbed through the thin phone book, studied the ads in the yellow pages, figuring out where she was.

"Miss, you can go now." The policeman stood in front of her. "We'll be deporting your friend in a few hours – he's asleep now. Of course, we'll need to confiscate the car."

Jill looked up, her hand holding the place in the phone book.

"If you don't mind waiting," he said, "I suppose I could give you a ride somewhere."

"I'm too close for a plane, too far away for a bus."

"Come get me when you decide."

Jill put the plane ride on her credit card, and still just barely got to work on time. She felt woozy, but hangovers didn't affect her anymore; she'd have drowned by now if they did.

Jill changed into her bathing suit, a solid black one-piece with no extra strings for fingers to grab, no frilly skirts that could get caught in fists. She looked at herself in the mirror. Gracie's teeth marks had faded into a small pink rose.

"Hi, Beautiful." Teresa appeared behind Jill.

She looked at Teresa in the mirror, without turning around. Teresa's glasses were already fogged in the locker room's stale, chlorine air.

"I called you this weekend, Jills, but you didn't pick up."

"Usual running around. Oh, I finally got rid of Daniel." Jill pulled up her bathing suit. "Sorry I missed you. Did you have fun?"

"Yeah, I guess."

"Well, let's go get Gracie. Bye, Mirror. Bye, Girls."

Teresa laughed and poked Jill's shoulder. "Cut that out."

Jill pulled Gracie to the middle of the pool and together they swam the width.

"You know, I almost left you," she whispered to Gracie. "I almost left you, but I charged a plane ticket, and now I'll be delivering fish for the next six months."

Gracie gurgled, paddling her arms in the warm water.

"I still might leave you," Jill said to Gracie, pulling her to the safety of the ladder.

The Nature of Sound (Had You Been Listening)

When I was in prison I sometimes listened to a radio station that no one else liked. The studio was just down the road from the prison, but even so, it was hard to hear at times, riding in on the breezes like dust or wisps of air. I wouldn't say fresh air. I would say odd air. Riding in through prison bars like wisps of odd air. And when it did waft into my radio, I never knew what I would hear. Sometimes jazz. Sometimes a muffled voice asking for a screwdriver because the damn tape drive was jammed. Or sometimes someone reading the news with such passion I thought my heart would break, even if the story was only about an election or a sewer spill. I don't talk much about the year I spent in prison. It doesn't matter much now. And my current friends don't even know about it. I've changed coasts, gained weight, joined the PTA. And I won't say that the station got me through a rough time or anything like that. Nothing got me through that time except time. There was all the noise. We were allowed radios. And everyone chose a radio station that was different from one another. Our only blast of individuality. The place was a mix of disco and punk (it was 1982 after all); you could hear the sounds vying for air space. There was soul and classic rock and fifties rock. All at an equal volume. It was all we had. And there was my little radio that sometimes played jazz and blues and news and was still committed to the revolution. That was the tag line. I don't think I was the only listener in the prison. But there couldn't have been many of us. For some reason, the men listened to it more. But that was only hearsay. On the women's side of things, the only time I heard news that wasn't screamed or shortened was on my little radio. Tin static. But there it was. I used to imagine what the announcers looked like based on their voices and their choice of music. I used to sketch them on notebook paper, because there wasn't much else to do. But I couldn't nail down the white girl. I was fascinated by her. We had a lot in common, I thought. Two white girls in seas of black faces. Well, where I was, there were a few other white girls. But I kept to myself. Where she was, as far as I could hear, there weren't any other white voices. She was actually a terrible DJ, but she kept me amused that year. I can still hear the earnest, musical way she signed on — "You are listening to WTPV in Johnsonville, North Carolina. I'm Rachel Goldstein," — full of promise, but then at a loss, as her voice faded out.

By the time I got the white reporter job, the station was already in decline. That is to say it was not my fault. The bed was on fire when I got into it.

I still don't know what made me so hell bent on moving to Johnsonville, North Carolina to work at WTPV – The People's Voice. Was it the dusty streets or the small-minded people? The boarded-up store fronts or the mangy stray dogs? The cloying taste of sweet iced tea? The lack of whole wheat bread? From a distance all of those things are charming, have their charm. They sing out like temptations; can you be sophisticated enough to forgo sophistications? To live amidst this barrenness and not complain? The answer was no. I could not. Jesus may have loved community cars, as the sign read on the car lot at the edge of town — Jesus Saves/Used Cars — but I could not.

Johnsonville was hidden in the folds of eastern North Carolina. Within those folds were one restaurant, five funeral homes (four for blacks, one for whites) and two radio stations. The white one played Christian country music from a double wide mobile home. And of course, WTPV played jazz and blues and news, and was still committed to the revolution.

I was the white reporter. Marcus was the black reporter. And Rene and Thad, who started the station, filled in all the other blanks. Thad was the engineer, and Rene was the whirlwind, running the station, producing children's shows and prison documentaries, filling in on Community Expressions when neither Marcus nor I could do the on-air interviews. We produced sounds for the poorest county in North Carolina. Sound has a life of its own. It remains in the air. Once words are uttered, they never disappear. Or so I used to think in those days. Our self-importance kept us going, kept us able to stay on the air for nineteen hours a day.

Almost every night, I had to broadcast the news, interview someone, then play jazz until the next volunteer arrived. Almost every morning when I got to the station, the news was crumpled around the AP Wire machine. In 1982, the news still came across on a real wire machine. It was a hulking metal box connected to a phone line, with a typewriter in its guts. It was intended to print ceaselessly, but ours always had fits and starts. Mostly it pounded loud, never-ending news.

This morning, yards of blank paper formed ribbons of beige paper down the hallway. Again, the ink had run out. There were yards of blank news. It had begun to fade around the baseball updates, and went paler and paler as the news ran on. By the time the international news update appeared there were only occasional blue letters until the ribbon ran out entirely. I cut the switch off and the machine shuddered to a halt, still trying to type out news until the last bit of electricity reached its keys. I reached in to change the ribbon. My hands were blue with ink by the time I finished. I flipped the switch on the AP Wire, and the news started printing again.

The first blobs of news came out smeared on the manila roll of paper. Impossible to read, but then, after a few paragraphs, it reverted to the regular pale blue letters. All the news looked the same in that pale blue type, but it was really a mixture. How could you determine what should be read and what should be thrown out? The deficit. Too tedious. A cat burglar — that is an actual cat who burgled, stealing shiny pieces of jewelry. Too cute. These were mixed in with various cancer breakthroughs that always made me cry, since I'd lost my dad to cancer, and mixed in with those were fledgling news stories about AIDS. There wasn't a name for it at first. It was just a disease that was affecting gay men. Today came the news that it affected gay men and Haitians. There were the letters — all caps, all in blue, buried in with all the other news about wars and fires and cats — spelling out this amazing new piece of information as if it weren't anything special. I ripped the news off the machine, carrying the roll to my desk.

My desk was awash with old news: clippings from the papers, magazines and newsletters that we subscribed to. This was all before the internet made collecting news easier, but denser. And it's always been a mess to sort out. That part hasn't really changed, I suppose. Though I don't pay as much attention now. I like silence. I like finding my news silently now. I rarely listen to the radio or turn on the TV. I don't even like music to infiltrate my thinking.

I swept the other news to the side and unfurled this afternoon's roll of news. I threw the cat burglar story in the trash along with a complicated story about the deficit. I couldn't figure out how to rewrite it. Not that we had to. As subscribers, we were licensed to rip the news straight from the AP Wire machine and read it unchanged. And I admit that there were days when I did just that. Rip the stories off the machine and drag them into the studio, reading exactly what the AP writers had written and posted to the wire. Word for fucking word. But not today. I had time. So today, I would rewrite the news as if it mattered.

The cancer story. Trash. Then I fished it out. I would be able to read it out loud without crying today. The AIDS story. I took my scissors and cut it out carefully, and started making little stacks of paper scraps. National stories in one stack. Local in another. I fished the cat burglar story out of the trash can. I needed to fill the time.

After I finished cutting out the stories, I went through to find actuality. I could call people in Durham or Raleigh or Chapel Hill to talk about the stories. I learned to use the list of academics or low-level politicians who would actually talk to us. Higher levels tended not to return our calls. I didn't really blame them. Who were we? Some odd station out in the boondocks, yet even odder still, with 100,000 watts of clear channel.

Who would I call about this new disease?

"Hey, Rene?"

She walked over, carrying her coffee and stacks of bills.

"Have you heard about this gay cancer?"

Rene leaned over my shoulder and read the story I had cut out. "I heard about it. But not much."

"Who should I call about it?"

"Try the list of doctors at Duke."

"Yeah, but it seems like there should be some specialist who would know more."

"I don't know. It just all seems so weird."

"It just seems so deliberate. You know? A disease that only affects gay men and Haitians."

"Try Hayden. He can usually talk about science."

"Yeah, but he's a moron."

I didn't call Hayden Stone because, well, he was a moron. He had a great radio voice, so I often used him. But if you listened carefully to what he had to say, you realized that it didn't add up to much. He never used sources. Just quoted "studies" and "facts."

I put the story in my stack of no actuality and proceeded to the chemical spill. I could call Hayden for that one.

I had seen the trucks myself. But I didn't know what I had witnessed.

"Hayden?"

I could picture him in his house. I'd been there once in Raleigh, trying to get a lengthier clip. There were stacks of newspapers, with a crooked pathway leading to the kitchen, the bathroom, the back porch. But more jolting was the body connected to that sonorous radio voice. I'd never seen anyone so mismatched. There he was in his overalls, crumbs from breakfast on the bib and of course in his beard.

"Hayden, it's Rachel from WTPV?"

"Rachel. A pleasure."

"What do you know about the PCBs that are popping up around here?"

"Well, I do know that PCBs are to be avoided."

"Hold on. Let me get this on tape."

I recorded his words, and I thanked him for his time. Okay. He was a moron. But he had a good radio voice. And his voice could interrupt my voice, giving us the illusion of texture.

Rene and Thad started WTPV in 1972. They had approached Alice Johnson in the spring, wanting to rent space to house the studios.

"Why in the world would you want to start a radio station out here in Johnsonville?" Alice stood in her doorway, not even letting them inside her house. It had been one of those hot spring days, portentous of a brutally humid summer to follow. Thad and Rene were patient. They both stood grinning, their 4-year-old, Sasha, in tow, starting to chase the cats that were sniffing her ankles.

"Well, we're from here. And there's a void," said Thad. Rene added, "Just imagine. Some other voices on the radio." Alice could see her neighbors peeking, pulling back their curtains to get a better look at the two black people on her porch. So, in a fit of irritation, she rented out the servants' quarters next door to her own house to Rene and Thad, where they were soon to establish WTPV.

Rene and Thad didn't move in right away. There was a lot of work to be done on the house, which was no great shakes to begin with. Servants' quarters weren't built that well. And these had never been maintained. Alice's father had put the carpet in, nailing it over the pine board floors. The rent from the building was always meant to be Alice's income, in case she never married, which she never did. The carpet had been nasty to begin with – green with winding vine strangling the nap.

Thad and Rene rented a steam cleaner from the A&P and did their best to make the carpet brighter. Alice watched them haul it up the stairs on the outside of the building, and a few hours later she watched them haul it back down, after they dumped gallons of murky brown water over the edge of the balcony. She told me that she tiptoed up later that afternoon, and as she suspected, the carpet looked no different. The vine was brown in places, the nap folded down.

The additions Rene and Thad put in place had actually made the building uglier: they had nailed green carpet to the walls like a vertical putt-putt range to make the rooms soundproof; they had drilled giant holes in the floor and snaked wires through them across the ceiling like bundled branches. The maid's bedroom was now the broadcast room, with giant egg crate mattresses on the walls, the tan-colored craters supposed to be collecting the sounds, keeping them from bouncing around the building.

The years had not been kind to the station. The same green carpet lined the walls, the egg crate valleys stained dark with years of sounds falling into their pits, and Alice's father's carpet still nailed to the floor, the vines barely perceptible anymore through footprints and dust.

Toxins trumped the gay cancer that night. For my interview show, I had invited an anti-nuclear activist from Raleigh. Brad Parsons was slim — unbelievably so — with close cropped blonde hair. What did it matter? We were on the radio, but I had developed a bad habit of sleeping with my interviewees. It was lonely in Johnsonville.

He was so serious. I tried to draw him out, just a few questions before we went live.

"There are toxins everywhere," he said. "It's not just nukes."

Should I spill the beans? Get my own story scooped? I decided I would. He could be my actuality. I was so sick of using Hayden.

"What do you know about the PCBs that are showing up around here?"

"I don't know much."

It wasn't much of a flirtation, but it would do. I sat at the board. We didn't have an engineer on duty, so I had to adjust the levels myself, spinning mysterious dials, pushing odd buttons. The national news feed was still on, so I didn't have much to do. As soon as that program was over, I announced our guest. Brad Parsons. Lanky. I didn't say that out loud. I put on a record, Oscar Peterson, giving myself some time before I went live.

"It must have taken you a long time to learn how to operate all those controls."

"I had to teach myself, actually. No one really had time to show me what to do."

Something in my brain told me that pride goeth before the fall. So I amended my bragging. "I'm still not perfect at it."

"You seem like you know what you are doing."

"It was really trial by fire."

Meanwhile, I noticed that I couldn't hear the music through the speakers. So I kept turning the volume up higher.

Pride goeth.

"I'm still not perfect."

Louder volume still.

"You look competent." Brad smiled. The flirting was working. Something to dull the small town boredom.

"Well, I guess I do feel proud of myself, a little."

And then my face went ashen.

"What's wrong?"

"Nothing."

I just realized that I had left the microphone on. I didn't say that to him. But had you been listening, you would have heard our flirting, heard the music get louder and louder. Heard me say that I still wasn't an expert at running the board. And the music would have gotten so loud on your radio that you would have heard the distortion.

I never told Brad that I'd left the mic on. We did the interview. Brad came home with me, stayed the night, and that was that.

One night I was listening to the station. My cellmate had been able to go to the rec room that night. And the music kept getting louder and louder until my little radio shook on its stand. Behind the music I could hear voices: How do you know how to work the board? How could you teach yourself? I'm not very good at it yet. No fucking kidding. That's why I listened to that station. I hadn't been good at writing bad checks. She wasn't good at radio. Somehow, we all just managed and mangled.

I wished she wouldn't spend so much time talking about poison. I don't care much about the PCBs she's reporting. The poison I deal with here is much stronger. I'm sure the water here is full of toxins, but there's water. So I don't complain. The water out there and the water in here is the same. Invisible. I turn on my radio and listen for other news. I'd rather listen to the griping or the stress or the mistakes. Those are funny. Marcus's war news and Rachel's poisons, well they're boring. And God forbid they discuss the economy. That's what got me here in the first place.

If I could call in, I'd tell her to be quieter. Not to bother about events she has no control over. Gay cancer. Why bother? Still, she makes me want to care, even though I don't. That earnest white voice. All alone. Like me. So I draw. And draw and draw and draw. I draw the women here, and they like that. What is it about seeing yourself that makes people smile? And when I draw, the other women leave me alone. And that's all I want.

It was no surprise that the station had no money. It was more of a surprise that it had managed to survive for ten years. Stations like WTPV relied on donors, grants, and underwriters. Here's where we blame Reagan, not me or Rene or Thad or Marcus. Had you been listening, you might have heard who to blame. Arts grants were drying up, people were becoming stingier, and there just wasn't that much commerce in the listening area that would underwrite us. So we remained poor. Poverty did beget poverty, and the station was no exception. The clutter added to the feeling of poverty, which fed upon itself. It was impossible to clean up - too many years of gathering data. Newspapers, magazines, press releases. We should have been able to throw things away, but we could not.

There was an apartment below the radio station. And that's where I lived. I shared it with the mice and the occasional rat. Alice used it to store old papers and junk mail she hadn't had time to go through. There wasn't much demand for the space – VISTA workers for the radio station, school teachers, me. But the others soon got tired of the constant drumming of the AP Wire machine. I found the thumping and droning to be my white noise. When Rene and Thad first installed the wire machine, it weakened the floor with its vibrations, worrying a hole into the ceiling and giving the mice better access. Alice supposed the floor boards had rotted over the years; Thad eventually stuck an old piece of plywood under the machine, and the hole in the ceiling was still there, but filled in. It muffled the sound a little, but not enough so that it couldn't be heard. The droning was steady, like the droning of the trucks near Alice's other rental.

The walls were sound absorbent, which meant that every sound had soaked into the thick green carpet that covered them. Of course, they couldn't talk, but I always wondered if the sounds that sank in could somehow be regenerated. By the time the sounds drifted down to my apartment under the studios, they were unintelligible. Perhaps they always were. That's just the nature of sound.

The next morning, when I saw the trucks again, they simply seemed to be leaking. When the trucks first started dumping the sludge by the side of the road, there weren't a lot of complaints. But no one realized that these were the trucks that were actually dumping carcinogens on our streets. It just seemed like the same leaky trucks or dribbling cars that always passed our way. So there was no need to take license plates. The poverty in the area made room for rickety cars and trucks. We were all too caught up in our day-to-day lives to notice the difference. They had farms to maintain, shifts to cover, houses to clean. We had to keep the radio station on the air for nineteen hours each day.

"Where's Marcus?" Thad was carrying stacks of cassettes that Marcus had filled and abandoned.

Rene answered, her hands fidgeting behind her back. Calculating. Who was going to get in trouble more? "He had to go to the A&P for something."

"When he gets back, tell him to see me."

Thad wasn't pleased. But he was the only one who could talk to Marcus. I'd gotten into a huge fight with Marcus early on, so I mainly steered clear of him when I could. The upshot was that he wouldn't have to broadcast the news with me, but would do it whenever I was sick or on vacation. Or he could do special stories. It wasn't fair, but neither was working with him, so in the interest of keeping my job, I agreed. I was too young to voice my objection. And there was the race thing too.

I couldn't articulate it. As the only white girl at the station, I felt exposed. Everyday to me was a constant reminder that I needed to prove that I wasn't racist. Yet how does anyone do that? Especially a 24-year-old who grew up in the south. Despite the years in Manhattan, I still felt unable to speak about it. Was it enough that I took a job where I was the only white staff member? Did that give me special privileges to talk about race? But I didn't know what those would be. Rene and Thad liked me. Marcus hated me. He saw me as a knee-jerk liberal, verging on racist. And according to Thad, he had barely contained his fists during our big argument. The volunteers were mostly black, too. A few white people from Durham came over to spin records or show off or play old Ella Fitzgerald cuts. There were donors of all colors. But mainly it was a black-run station. A true community station. And I wasn't really a part of the community. I was an outsider. As a southern Jew, I thought I would be used to that. But there was constantly Marcus.

Marcus was another one who didn't really match his voice. He had a voice smooth like butter, but a body that had been in prison and was both built up and wracked. Muscles and scars. I tried to hide from him the fact that I didn't know what I was doing.

I had a gut sense of what the news was. I knew that if you read the right stories and got someone to make a comment about them, you could do a decent newscast. I was okay at gathering news if there were no deadlines. I didn't like deadlines. I preferred instead to mull things over, listening to the tapes repeatedly, letting people's voices trail off. They reminded me of songs and poetry that didn't fit into a newscast, but did make for interesting listening in those days. Maybe we're heading back to that now, the odd juxtaposition of words and music. But who listens? Who listened then, anyway? I always suspected that the liberals from Durham and Raleigh who sent us money didn't really listen. But that was okay. I used their voices from time to time, which they liked. The radio station sort of wove these voices together. And sometimes there was news worthy of reporting. And sometimes we were actually the ones to report it.

Though how four people could actually run a radio station, even with volunteers, baffled me.

Marcus finally arrived around 4:00 p.m., just in time to sign the volunteer out and help me read the news. Our relationship had been testy from the start, but separate ever since he had tried to throw me out a window.

I didn't know why he hated me so much. Or I did, but I just accepted it.

I had even let him use my bathtub when we first moved to town. We were hired together after all. Somehow he hadn't been able to get his electricity turned on so he could have hot water. So, I let him use my old clawfoot tub. Afterward, I tried to find out why it was that my hot water worked and his didn't. He looked around confidentially.

"Racism."

Later it turned out that he hadn't paid the $200 deposit to Duke Power, which in a roundabout way was sort of racist, but not in the way he meant. He was trying to tell me that the electric company turned my power on and not his, solely on the basis of our skin color.

And could I buy that?

It was 1982. It wasn't too far-fetched. But it wasn't plausible either. After all, the town was 65% black. Somebody had to have hot water. When it came to light that it was $200, not skin color that made the difference, I took it upon myself to talk to him about it. It was stupid looking back. Why should I have bothered? I'd never bother now.

"It's the $200." I told him. "It's the money, not the color."

"It's the same thing."

"No, it isn't. It's class. Not race."

"Are you saying you are of a better class than me?"

"No." Lord.

But that was the end of our relationship. Or rather that was the beginning of his hating me. And my inability to come to terms with it.

"You are not entitled to hot water."

"I'm not? I think I am." He folded his arms and I could have sworn he made fists, but who knows any more? It felt threatening, but I was too stupid to realize. I kept pursuing it, trying to make him understand it from my perspective.

"If you can't afford to pay, you tell them. And then you fill out a form. And then, they'll turn on your power."

"But that's not the point. I bet if you went in there without your $200, they would have still turned on your electricity."

"But I didn't. I paid the money. I got the electricity. Simple."

"Not simple."

"Why not?"

"Suppose I don't have the money."

"But you do."

"Actually, I don't. Can I borrow it from you?"

"No. Umm maybe. I can see if I have it."

But Marcus was laughing. "Got ya."

I didn't realize liberal guilt could be so amusing or infuriating. That was hardly the worst of our arguments. We argued over how to pronounce names. Moss - Cow. Moss - Coe. We argued over Reagan. He was worse than Carter. There was no difference. We argued over the weather. Really. I didn't think you could argue over the weather, but we managed to disagree over whether you should rewrite a weather report or not. They all sound the same. I still think they should all sound the same. It's weather. It's not supposed to sound different from what the AP Wire writes. And the day Marcus almost threw me out the window, we were arguing over whether we should cover Vice President Bush's trip to Raleigh. Me: No. Marcus wanted to borrow my car.

"I just don't think that's our niche. Don't you think that other news agencies will be there?"

"But we deserve a place too."

"But we're not real news."

"I'm real. You're real. I think." And that's when he picked me up and held me halfway out the window. And that's when I realized that even though I might be right, it didn't matter if someone was holding me over traffic. What traffic there was, anyway, in Johnsonville.

I screamed. But it didn't matter. Thad and Rene were too busy to notice. And the volunteer was tucked in tight in the studio, door shut. I screamed again. Marcus laughed.

"Shit. I'm not going to throw you out. I need your car."

I laughed too, but I wasn't so dumb not to know that it was a turning point. I handed him my keys.

As it turned out, he didn't even get close enough to hear Bush. He got some crowd noise, some activists protesting. Which, actually, as it turned out, sounded pretty good.

Since then, he'd been in a better mood around me, almost as though we could pretend we had reached an understanding.

"Hey Rachel." Marcus tossed me a cassette. "You might find this interesting."

"What is it?"

"News."

I rolled my eyes. He continued. "Something you might find interesting. Give me credit if you use it."

"What is it?"

"Just listen. Streeter – the old guy who hangs out by the A&P - saw them dumping something out on 43 last night, just like you said."

"So?"

"So, it might be useful."

"Or not."

Marcus smiled and headed back to his office.

"Wait. How did you even find out about this?"

"Some people like to tell me things, too."

"Oh."

I put the cassette in the recorder and listened. Most of the tape was static, too many road noises to be useful. Streeter had a good radio voice too though. I had to give Marcus that. The two of them bantered about weather and jails they had seen, liquor they had tried, weed they had smoked. As an interview technique, it wasn't bad. Certainly it established a level of trust for the interviewee at least, if not the listener. For me, it was sort of interesting. The pride Marcus took in having been incarcerated. I suppose it was something to have survived. I don't think I could have survived that. Even being in an office was a sort of prison for me. The idea of not having room to move made my heart pound.

I didn't expect to have a breaking news story. That wasn't really my job. I felt it was more to report things that didn't always get reported. I didn't see myself finding that great missing link to a story. I saw myself slowly plodding away. Ripping a story, finding someone to talk about it, reading it over the air. That sort of thing. So, when Marcus presented me with evidence, as he called it, I only wanted to see if it would match a story. After all, it was no secret that the water here was nearly undrinkable. High levels of PCBs and other toxins had been found in almost all the water tables this far north in the state. But it was hard to trace. Industries came and went here: cotton, tobacco, furniture. Most of it was defunct. Shells of industry and busted unions.

But here was Marcus's mole: an old drunk. His words slurred on the tape, but it was very clear what he saw:

"A white van. Dumped barrels of something that looked like Kool-Aid on the side of the road."

Well, the testimony of a drunk passed out in a pumpkin patch wouldn't hold much sway. But he'd had no reason to lie.

I called Hayden, since I could no longer call Brad.

"Hey, Hayden. What would be the likelihood of catching someone dumping chemicals off of Route 43?"

"Possible. Unlikely. What do you have?"

I told him. "Hey, be on the lookout for something to corroborate. Thanks."

Marcus might have been in earlier that afternoon, but he was gone long before it was time to actually read the news. All of our planning was for naught. The carefully sorted stacks. One square stack for me. One for him. Suddenly, he had an interview that couldn't wait. Of course, these things can't wait. And even though I should have been angry, I really wasn't. After all, what difference did it make? I might read a little more tonight. We had scripted it again, and I had my pick. I could skip the stories about Russia. I really didn't feel like reporting on the Cold War. By 1982, the Cold War was the stuff of spy novels and bad television. And if I didn't want to report on it, I didn't have to.

It was very liberating to be in charge of reading the news. If I subscribed to the idea that no one was listening, it didn't matter whether I reported on the Cold War or not. If I subscribed to the idea that the only people listening were people in prisons and mental institutions, then they could be free to pick and choose their news as well. They might hear more details later, from someone else. But from me, they weren't going to hear about an ongoing non-war, designed to terrify. They didn't need more terror. They had enough just being imprisoned. And if I subscribed to the idea that people listened to us out of sympathy, then those people certainly got their news from other sources. Newspapers were still fat in 1982, with stories that went on for pages.

The national news feed was still playing when I sat down at the microphone. They could report on the Cold War if they wanted to. It was sort of expected. They needed to explore the Cold War until it ended. It was a daily feed. Missiles here and there. From us, from them. The boats were still returning from the Falklands. It seemed like people thrived on these wars. Almost a need to know that there was warfare in our midst. And yet, they weren't fantastical, because people had died. I supposed that spies really did go back and forth to Russia. And some of them were killed as well. Maybe it was wrong to be a pacifist reporter. I couldn't take any of it seriously.

The national news feed ended on a light note. Children reporting on their summer plans. That was supposed to segue into the local reportage. But how could I segue from children talking about TV and hopscotch to this new disease that hadn't settled on a name. I put on Ahmad Jamal. Jazz was the great segue. It could lead from one set of emotions to another. From one catastrophe to the next. Or on a more light-hearted day, from one piece of fluff to the next.

Had you been listening, you would have heard the national news in all its smoothness segue from the Cold War to children playing, without noticing the shift. You would have heard the clunk of my needle on the record as I tried to find an equally smooth shift, but knowing it was impossible, I would have simply jumped from the national version of the news to my record. And you would have heard a few minutes of jazz, of McCoy Tyner, because a jazz piano can mean anything. And then you would have heard me say, "In local news...." What happened? It hardly changed. A school superintendant was fired. One was hired. Land was set aside for a park. Land was set aside for an industrial park. I loved that term.

In New York, I had eaten lunch in Exxon Park. Concrete all around with a fake waterfall dousing the side of the building. Here in North Carolina, they built industrial parks. They were just old farms, turned into office buildings, spread so far apart that everyone needed a car to get from one complex to another. Maintenance workers rode in golf carts to spread more fertilizer over the vast expanse than the land had seen when it was farmed. It wasn't sustainable. But it had such a nice name. The words industrial and park could merge, creating a complex meaning. Like cold and war.

So, I read about the new industrial park that was being envisioned off of route 40. It would join Raleigh and Durham and maybe even spread east. In the same breath, I read a press release — unfiltered — from the local Sierra Club, moaning about the new industrial parks. There were trees at stake, animals at risk, whole habitats that would be wiped out.

And, even though the national news had touched on the new gay cancer, I read another story about it. One person. One event. I even had tape from the local lesbian and gay alliance spokeswoman. She was questioning. It didn't seem real.

Privately, we wondered. How could a disease target gay men and Haitians? She and I spoke candidly before I recorded her. Her recording was bland. Our conversation was not. We were coming up with conspiracies. We wondered how the disease could transmit. We knew nothing and speculated everything. It seems so quaint now.

With all we know about the disease. But then, it was scary. It was starting to hit our friends. And no one knew how to keep it from spreading or to keep from getting it. Who knew when the gay men/ Haitian gate would open? Would any of us with contact with gay men contract the disease? She and I speculated. We cursed. And yet in the end, all I had was a few seconds of her asking for more research. That's what you heard, had you been listening.

I was glad Marcus wasn't there. He didn't like the new disease. He wouldn't say that he didn't like gay people, but it was clear that the news of this disease didn't move him the way it moved me. So, I took advantage of his absence, and I read more about the disease. I nixed the Cold War in favor of the strangeness of a new epidemic. It was mostly repetition. But perhaps it didn't matter.

And then I read the weather again. People need the weather. They like to hear it over and over. We didn't have traffic, didn't subscribe to a traffic report. Our news kept you on your toes, because you never knew what was going to come next. What grand mistake we might make next. Me keeping a mic on long after I had run out of things to say. Mispronunciation. Misspeak. I think it kept people awake on long drives or in traffic. We provided a service. It kept you entertained if you were in prison. It kept your sanity, maybe, if you were in the mental institution. After all, if the people on the outside sounded crazy, perhaps there was hope for you.

Had you been listening you would have heard the scratch in my voice. The constriction in my throat. Rain. Heavy at times. It was all heavy at times. The rain, the news. Had you been listening, you would have heard me read the weather with the foreboding of a gypsy: the rain will be heavy at times. You will feel its downpour and be drenched. Of course, I was speaking for myself. The overcast conditions. Yet, I offered the promise that the rain would only be heavy at times. Other times, there might be sun breaks. But who knew. It was my job to warn.

Rachel sounded dire. That's not why I listen. I'm serious enough. I don't need warnings anymore. I ignored them before, at any rate.

It hadn't been a good scheme in the first place. We were broke, but who wasn't? Randy made it sound so easy. You just write the one check. It's just a little more than you have in your account. And by the time they find out, you close the account and start over. We didn't clear much that way. It was just a few extra dollars here and there. New accounts, other banks, other stores. Just a little bit over. "They deserve it, Roberta," Randy said. They deserve it. What did we do with the extra money? Who knows? A new

*television, a new radio, a weekend at the beach. I didn't even have my kids
then. That might have justified it, buying milk for starving children, writing
bad checks. But no. Randy said, "They would believe a woman more." He
couldn't possibly write the checks. They check the IDs closer on a man. They
care more when a man writes a check. But a woman. A woman writes a
check, and everyone trusts her. And so, I wrote bad checks for the both of us.
    Sometimes Randy came to visit, but not often. The prison was hard to get
to. And I admit, I was hard to reach those days, too. It was just so damned
loud in there. The visiting area was full of kids, shrieking, crying, or sitting
sullenly. Their silence was worse. You could hear it reverberating off their
mothers. And I couldn't talk when I saw that. So, Randy came down a couple
times. I do think he was sorry that I ended up in prison. I don't think he was
sorry that he didn't. But all in all, how would you ever get back together with
somebody after that? So, we didn't promise to wait for each other. Basically,
I just waited for him to leave. His last visit, we were both silent. And then
he left. I really didn't want him to come back. I mean, it could break the
monotony, but the awkwardness was worse. So, I listened. And I waited for
the day when I could choose silence.*

I signed off – You've been listening to WTPV in Johnsonville,
North Carolina, I'm Rachel Goldstein – and let my voice trail off.
I went home to my mice. Mouse droppings were already over the
kitchen table and chairs. Fortunately, they weren't in my bedroom.
So I changed into my jammies and went to sleep.

The next morning, the station was a little too quiet. The mid-
morning volunteer hadn't shown up, and the early morning volunteer
had to go to work. I filled in, putting on Joe Pass.

I checked the AP machine, and that's when I found out I'd been
scooped.

What a shock it was to see in print what we'd been suspecting all
along: Deliberate, large scale dumping. PCBs were found all along
the highway from Johnsonville to South Bend. The article over the
AP was brief and terse. Higher levels of PCBs were found on our
highway. No idea who had dumped them. Could have been anyone
along the east coast.

It seemed too deliberate — picking the poorest county in the state
and dumping chemicals. Streeter was right. Had I gone with the story
of the old drunk, I would have had the story first. But I was oddly
relaxed about it. I didn't have the skills to dig up the perpetrator. I
didn't have a lab to test the chemicals. So it was good that someone
else did. My job was simply to talk about what other people had

dug up. And maybe use my own sources to comment. Nothing too complex.

Nothing too complex. That was what I ran on. Completely out of my element here.

The night volunteer didn't show up again. I could cover for almost anyone, except Tony B, who played the widest variety of blues. I could improvise on jazz. But whenever I had to cover for Tony B, people called in and complained. Fortunately, tonight, I was just covering for a white volunteer from Durham. His jazz picks were easy to reproduce. The other explanation was that no one was listening, or if they were, they had no access to phones.

Tonight I was only playing dead musicians. At night, it's easy to fall into the reverie with dead musicians. There is something haunting about what they've left us. I lay down on the floor of the album room, trying to nap. Coltrane had nice long songs that let me sleep. "Stardust" lasts seventeen minutes – enough to remember Coltrane's life, pick out another album, lay my head on the carpet.

Dead musicians crowded my thoughts. I was supposed to play Monk and Air Song or whoever else modern and past, but I found myself gravitating toward the dead ones. This radio station, this community voice collective, prided itself on the most recent jazz, or the rarest cuts. But tonight all I wanted to hear was John Lennon. His voice haunted me. There weren't many people I mourned in such a direct way. Of course there are political martyrs, but they didn't leave music, and their iconic status gives them a statuesque finish. It's the musicians who seem that they're still alive. You can hear the speeches, and the scratchy voices. But they don't echo in the same way as the music does. I knew Marcus would tease me, and Rene and Thad would chastise me, but probably not fire me.

My tendency to play the music of dead white people wasn't enough to let me go. It was hard to find anyone who would come to Johnsonville, this remote spot on a map, who would report the news for so little money. It wasn't impossible, so I was a bit careful. I wasn't the last of my kind, but there were more and more women, ever since Reagan, wearing little silk scarves tied at the neck and using feminism that way. Oh, there were still people who would work this hard for this little money. But I assumed there was safety in inertia. So I grabbed Lennon, and more Coltrane for good measure, and hoped that no one had their radios on.

In the middle of the night, right before I was going to sign off, I looked through the studio window. I saw the truck again. In the moonlight, it was clear that it was intentional. It wasn't a broken truck, as I had thought before. It seemed to spread a deliberate trail as it wound its way through town.

I shut down the station and went downstairs to the mice. I had to face my situation. It wasn't healthy, living with mice. They nibbled my cereal and left their droppings on my shelves. I ended up keeping all my food in the fridge, even though it turned the bread stale. I needed a cat.

The cat was going to change everything. A cat could take care of loneliness and kill mice at the same time.

Rene told me about the house in the middle of town with 200 cats. I was sure she was exaggerating, but when I got there, I thought she might not be. She told me that when the kindergarten children were learning to count, they went to this house to count cats.

So Rene took me to Mrs. Madsen's old farmhouse off Highway 43 to pick out a cat. I'm sure there were at least fifty cats in the tall grass in front of her house. Tabbies, black cats, long haired white cats, semi-Siamese. They circled our ankles and clawed at our calves. Grabbing one was like bobbing for apples. I bent down, ignoring the clawing and the mewing, and pulled up a silver tabby. Susan. A human name would put her on equal footing with me. But it didn't work that way.

Susan didn't like being cooped up in my apartment. She battled me for the exits and shredded my towels. She knocked over my dish drainer, sending all the glass shattering to the floor. She did kill mice, though finding their squeaking, bloody bodies wasn't the solution I had been looking for. I wanted them scared, not tortured.

And she brought in fleas. I realized I had to get her to a vet.

There were more veterinarians in Johnsonville than banks. It was such a tiny, skewed town. I suppose when the horses outnumber the people, then vets are in high demand. Johnsonville seemed to be a breeding ground for the horse trade in Tryon, further south. The flatness made it as suitable for horses as for tobacco farms.

Only one vet could see me right away. And given the state of Susan's health — the matted fur, the fleas — I decided that I would see him. After all, I could switch to someone more in demand later.

The office was tidy. A small woman was at the front desk, covered in fur. It was all over her clothes and her face, even in her hair. She didn't seem to mind.

"This is that horrible cat I called about this morning."

The receptionist smiled.

"Maybe she's not acting up in here, but she's already shredded my curtains and peed on my clean laundry."

I filled in the paperwork and waited in the reception area.

The receptionist came away from her front desk and led me to the exam room. There seemed to be only one. When the vet walked in, I had to hide my surprise. I'm sure I didn't do a good job, but I wasn't expecting the vet to be black. Up until that moment, it hadn't occurred to me that there weren't many black vets.

I handed him my flea-ridden kitty.

He took her gently, and with both hands, hefted her, looked at her underbelly.

"Did you get this cat from Mrs. Madsen?"

"How could you tell?"

Dr. Broome pinched the tabby's ear. "See that scratch?"

I leaned in.

"They're all damaged that way. Most people who get their cats around here pull them from out of her yard."

"She gave me permission."

At that point, he laughed. "Of course she did! You think she wants 200 cats?"

"Are there that many?"

"At last count. You know, they take the first graders to her house to learn to count —"

"Right. They learn to count by counting cats."

"You heard that too."

"Is it true?"

"As true as anything is in this town."

Here we were in the tiny sterilized office. The chair was obviously a hand-me-down. I had always assumed that vets were rich, but this obviously wasn't the case.

There was his diploma. He'd gone to vet school at Tuskegee. And now that I thought about it, I'd never met another black vet. All the ones from my childhood had been middle-aged white men. I didn't remember any women, either, though I certainly knew of a couple in New York. They seemed rich. But at the time, everyone seemed rich to me. I was in that phase when I prided myself on not making much money, but in reality, it wasn't pleasant. It gave me a feeling of self-importance, which didn't let me buy new shoes or even a decent coat.

The cat scale was gleaming though. Stainless steel. Susan squirmed on it.

Dr. Broome's voice was deep – maybe I could think of a way to get him on the radio.

"She's hefty. Especially for one of Madsen's cats. Eleven pounds and she's not even full grown."

"Oh? She doesn't seem that big to me."

"That's because she's not full grown. You're going to have to watch her."

Susan clawed Dr. Broome at that moment, and we both laughed.

"As I was saying..."

"So, can you fix her up? I assume she needs shots. I don't think Mrs. Madsen does very much for these cats."

"Of course."

"How long will it take, though? I have to do the news at five."

"Right. That's you. I recognized your voice."

"You listen to us?"

"What else would a black man listen to in this town? What kind of question is that?"

I couldn't tell if he was joking or not. Susan was in Dr. Broome's hands now. She deserved to be left on the street, I thought, but I'd never do that. She destroyed my only nice pair of pants, shattered my wine glasses, and even though they didn't match, I still needed them. She kept me up late at night between her howling and her chasing rats. But she also needed company, and since I did too, I kept her. Paid her vet bill. Got her her shots.

I only had ten minutes before I had to read the news. Tonight would simply be ripping and reading. I wondered if anyone noticed when it was my voice or simply the AP machine telling me what to say.

That night, long after I had finished the news and gone to bed, Susan started howling. This was different. It was a deep howl, and she was kicking her back legs. It was two a.m., and in my sleep-deprived haze, I realized that she was in heat. How long until morning? Somehow we dozed together until dawn. And there were still two hours to go.

At 8:00 a.m., I called Dr. Broome's office. The receptionist was out of breath, but pleasant as always. I could picture the fur flying off her hands as she answered the phone.

"Can you spay a cat when she's in heat?'

"Yes."

"Can you spay her today? I mean, right now?"

Cathy laughed. "Sure. I think Dr. Broome has an opening this afternoon."

"Can I drop her off now? If I don't, she may not live."

Fortunately, Cathy laughed again. "We can give her something to calm her down. Bring her on by."

The trip to Dr. Broome's wasn't as harrowing as it had been previously. Susan only jumped at the window twice. Most of the time, she just jumped from the backseat to the front. She stayed away from my arms this time, so I could drive less erratically. After two years in New York, not driving, my driving was erratic anyway, but having a wild cat in my lap made it worse.

"Here." I said to Cathy. I put Susan on the counter, resting one hand on her back.

Cathy grabbed a cardboard container, and without getting scratched, placed Susan inside. I was impressed.

Dr. Broome came out to see us. He had to stoop down to make eye contact with me. "So this is Susan again."

Susan had gone back to howling and stamping her back feet.

"Can you make it stop?" I asked.

"Not a problem. Someone just canceled, so we can do the surgery this morning. I'll keep her overnight. That way, you don't have to worry about her while you are doing the news."

I was relieved, but worried about the cost, of course. And I didn't know how to ask without appearing like I didn't care about the cat. I figured we'd arrive at a compromise. I could pay it off in bits if need be. My brother had given me a credit card, which I didn't like to use, but in this case I would.

Cathy brought it up first. "It will cost about $80. We have a payment plan."

"How could you tell that I need one?"

"I can always tell."

So, I left Susan with Cathy and Dr. Broome. I drove home first. It would be a couple hours before I would have to start gathering news. I took the opportunity to sweep the house. The mice had taken the opportunity to come out of the walls with Susan gone. I also found more shards of glass that I'd missed before. And then I had to mop. A cat in heat makes a mess.

I picked up Susan in the morning. Cathy wasn't there, and Dr. Broome was at the desk filling in for her.

"Where's Cathy?"

"She's sick."

"What will you do?"

"It's okay. I don't have many patients scheduled today."

Dr. Broome went in the back to get Susan. "You don't need to pay today. You can wait for Cathy to get back."

"Thanks. But that makes me feel bad."

Dr. Broome laughed. "No. We trust you for some reason. Maybe it's because you are on the radio."

I smiled. "I wish more people listened, then."

"Oh, you have quite the base."

"Not really, I mean we have the prison. And the mental hospital. They listen. Most people don't, I think. And I think that the people who want to listen to us can't always hear us."

"Smarter words were not said."

"Right. I mean it's the wind, though. Sometimes the wind blows the signal the right direction, and sometimes it doesn't."

"Again. Smarter words not said."

Dr. Broome gave me directions for taking care of Susan. Rest. I didn't ask how you make sure a cat rests. Medicine. That would be a challenge. Squirting liquid down Susan's throat. Wear gloves, he advised. Drink wine. And a follow up visit in a week to take the stitches out. I didn't ask whose.

I had to follow up the next morning though, because Susan had taken her own stitches out during the night. I thought she had disemboweled herself. I didn't even call first. I put Susan in her cardboard box with a towel and headed back to Dr. Broome's. Cathy was back, but I could tell she still didn't feel well. Her eyes were red. The fur was clinging to her hair. It looked like she didn't care this morning.

"I think Susan disemboweled herself," I said as I put her and her cardboard box on the counter.

I waited while Dr. Broome stitched her back up. When he brought her out to me, she had a collar on. It looked like a giant, plastic ruff.

"We'll keep her here for a couple days."

"I can't afford that." How embarrassing, that those were the first words out of my mouth. I felt like a fraud. I had a job, after all, but it didn't pay much. And I had no savings.

Cathy shook her head and told me not to worry about it. Payment plan. But I didn't want to afford it. I already hated this cat.

I worried about the cat when I got to the station. I worried about paying for her surgery; I worried about seeming like I didn't want to take care of her. I worried about paying for her new set of stitches; and I worried again about not wanting to pay for them.

Marcus was already there. Remarkably, he was cutting the news into squares for us. He was actually working, and I must have looked startled.

"Hey. Just pulling my weight," he said.

"Did I look surprised?"

"Yes." He looked up from his task. "I probably haven't been fair to you. But you fall into every liberal trap out there."

"Probably I do." I took a stack of news from him and started reading. I did not want to have this conversation. I'm white. He's not. I knew I fell into every trap, and I didn't want to be reminded of it. I thought I was doing pretty well, actually, of not saying anything racist, which usually meant, around Marcus, of not saying much at all. I was too afraid that whatever would come out of my mouth might be misconstrued.

So I sat next to him, and cut more news into squares.

"How should we do this tonight?" I asked. "Do you want to read first, or should we go back and forth?"

"I like it when we take turns telling the news." So we each took a stack of stories and picked the ones that we wanted to read. It was the most we had done together for months.

And that night, as we read, it actually went well. I wonder if people who were listening could tell when we'd worked together well, and when we'd been fighting. Of course they could. But they didn't bother to tell us. Most of the time.

The people in the prison wrote to us the most. I wondered what we sounded like to them. To be stuck in prison, listening to an odd radio station, seemed like a worse deal. But maybe it was better than listening to elevator music or pop. Maybe the uncertainty of what you'd hear on WTPV made a difference in your day. How could every day be the same if your radio station made it different? Would the announcers screw up? More often than not. If so, how badly?

There was the time that Rene announced that she was Thad. I wasn't there yet, but it was part of the station's lore. She turned on a tape that Thad had made. He announced, "I'm Thad Marshall." Then Rene replied as soon as she opened her mic, "And I'm Thad Marshall." Not Rene Marshall, who she was. But Thad Marshall, who, of course, she wasn't. I wish I had been there for it. Even thinking about it made me laugh. How did anyone trust us, if we didn't know our names? How does anyone trust any word heard on the radio? Sublimation. The sound just flies out the window through the air and wires. And sometimes it's heard, and sometimes it's not.

Later, I called to see how Susan was doing. Fine. Drugged. Her stitches were starting to re-heal. I couldn't figure out how someone could disembowel herself by accident. Was the cat suicidal or simply stupid? There was no answer.

"I heard your show last night," Dr. Broome was saying.

"Oh no."

"No, it was good. I like McCoy Tyner."

"Me too. I find him calming. No matter what kind of news I'm reading, he seems to fit."

"What kind of news was that, anyway?" Dr. Broome didn't sound mean, but he definitely noticed that it hadn't been a normal newscast, as if we had any normal newscasts.

"What do you mean? You mean the lack of any structure? I leave that to the national news people. They can have structure. We just read what makes sense for the area."

"No, don't get defensive. You just seemed to jump around a lot."

"I always jump around a lot. It's impossible to fill thirty minutes with local news. And most of the non-profits around know that we'll read whatever they send us, so we try to match it all up. It didn't work last night?"

"It worked fine. Just jumpy."

I suppose that if that was the worst criticism, I could stand it. My news was jumpy. My cat was stupid. I let the phone slip down.

Dr. Broome spoke first. "I didn't mean to hurt your feelings."

"No. It's not that." The real problem was that I didn't know what I was doing, but how do you admit that to someone? Reading news when I didn't know what to read. Reading weather when I needed to fill in.

"I like your newscast."

"Really?"

"Yeah, I really do. It's jumpy, but it's real. You never know what you're going to say next."

"I don't know what I'm doing." I couldn't believe I'd just said that. "I didn't just say that."

Dr. Broome laughed. "I won't tell anybody. That's why we listen. True community radio."

When I came by to pick up Susan, Cathy had already left. The doors were locked, and I was afraid I would have to spend the money to keep Susan there one more night.

Dr. Broome answered the door. He still had his white coat on, but he was clearly ready to leave. "I was waiting for you."

"I'm sorry. I thought you would be open a little longer." Marcus was sorting the news for me so that I could pick up Susan. Who knew what I would come back to? Marcus was so much about war. Cold wars, wars in Africa, aftermath of wars in the Falklands, aftermath of wars even from WWII. It didn't matter. If it was about war, it was important. I could argue with him. And some nights I did. But since he was doing me a favor, I had to go with it.

Dr. Broome handed me Susan. She was back in her cardboard box, and she had the big white cone over her head. She looked angry.

"Can I leave her at home while I read the news?"

"By herself? Not a great idea. She's got the buster collar on, but she could still try to get her stitches out again. And she looks mad."

"I can see that."

"You could bring her to the station, if you wanted. Go ahead and take the collar off. She should be okay in her box. And she'll be drugged still until you finish reading."

"Thanks. I hope this works. I guess nothing could happen, then."

"I'll be listening just in case. Oh, and I'll have Cathy send you a bill."

"That would be great. She said you have a payment plan?"

"Not a problem."

Dr. Broome helped me load Susan into my little car. He figured out the handle on the back door quickly, so I didn't have to explain to him how to jiggle it up and down, then pull hard. He didn't seem to be embarrassed for me about it. I couldn't be embarrassed about it. Local news at a local community radio station dedicated to doing good works. That pretty much insured a beat-up car with door handles that didn't work. It insured a payment plan for a sick cat, too, which he seemed okay with.

So, I brought Susan to the station with me. The first few minutes were fine. Marcus had indeed sorted the news, heavy on war, but he had left early. A note. An important interview of course.

I put on McCoy Tyner. How could I not if Dr. Broome was listening?

I started reading through the stacks of news. After the second war story about Namibia, I heard Susan begin to scratch. After the third story, Susan began scratching louder. And after the fourth story about a war in another part of Africa, Susan was scratching so hard that her box began to move across the floor.

She also started growling. It was a deep-throated growl, so loud, that I could see the needles pick it up on the monitor.

Had you been listening, you would have heard my accounting of wars in Africa. Then you would have heard scratching that started quietly, but then got louder and louder, until you heard the thumping of a cardboard box against the console. Before I had a chance to turn off the microphone, you would have heard a low growl at the same sound level as a voice. By this time, I was too surprised to keep reading, so you would have heard my voice replaced by the loud deep growling of a cat in prison. You would have heard me curse, though, right before I turned the microphone off and turned McCoy Tyner back on.

My heart was pounding. And the phones lit up. Rene on line one.
"What the hell is going on down there?"
"Nothing. I'll get it under control. This record will last for another five minutes."
"Okay, but this doesn't sound good."
When did I ever sound good?
Marcus on line two.
He was laughing too hard to speak. "What the hell is going on down there?"
"I thought you had an important interview."
"They didn't show up."
"Right."
"Who is that?"
"My cat."
"I won't ask."
"Don't. And I've got to fix this. Bye."
I went over to Susan. Now that she had clawed a hole in the box, she seemed happier. She couldn't fit her body through the hole yet, so she was still busy clawing. But just seeing outside the box seemed to calm her down. At least she wasn't clawing at her stitches anymore. Maybe she realized that it was impractical. At any rate, she was only going for the cardboard box. I could start crying. Or I could start laughing. Or I could do both. I didn't know how to calm the cat down. I had to fill twenty more minutes with news. And I couldn't just play jazz to fill the time. Both my boss and my coworker were listening for me to completely screw up. I gave Susan the can of tuna fish that I had bought for her coming home present. I just had to hope that she wouldn't try to disembowel herself again, at least not in the span of time that I had to fill. The tuna seemed to keep her occupied.

I opened the microphone and began to read. More war. But Susan was happy, and now the studio smelled like fish. I promised the weather and put on John Coltrane. Not "Stardust" — that was just for long emergencies. I just needed a few minutes to make sure Susan would behave. I hoped that the volunteer who was next wouldn't be late.

I could barely hear the knocking on the outside door. But after I patted Susan, it became louder. The door was always open for the next volunteer, so I couldn't figure out who would be stopping by after hours who didn't know this.

It was Dr. Broome. He was smiling.
"I heard Susan on the radio, and I thought you might need a hand."

"Jesus. Thank you. You're not the only person who heard Susan. I might have lost my job, tonight. Except that, well, I don't know who else would want this job."

Dr. Broome smiled again. He was much older than me, but it didn't matter. He was taking me seriously, sort of. "Where is she? I think I can cat-sit until you are finished."

"That would be great."

Dr. Broome picked up Susan. She immediately settled down. I finished reading the news. The volunteer showed up and Dr. Broome and I left together.

"Do you want me to help you get Susan home?"

"I'd like that," I said, "But my house is rampant with mice. It's embarrassing."

"If you aren't embarrassed by what happened tonight —"

"Oh, but I am."

"Well, you should be." We laughed. I didn't mind being insulted. I deserved it. I let a cat disrupt the news. At least I got the weather in. And the volunteer took over with music that was more modern, but harder to listen to.

Had you been listening, you would have heard wars and wars and caterwauling. And you would have heard easy but complex jazz like John Coltrane, followed by jazz from the volunteer that wanted you to work at what you heard. Lonnie did that all the time. People complained, but he insisted it was good for them. "You have to work for your jazz," he'd say. So, if you were in prison, you heard a cat gain freedom, and maybe that was gratifying.

I'll be able to sleep tonight: they're putting cats on the radio. There's always comfort in absurdity. Most of us can't sleep here. Or at least can't sleep at night. It's wrong, being told when to sleep, when to wake. If only to have a little bit of volition, we do things backwards. Wide awake, I worry. What will I do when I get out? It's not a question we ask during the day. Plans are a wasteland. It's too dangerous to think ahead. What if you come back? What if life outside isn't any different? What if you get out, only to find a larger prison around you? That's impossible we tell ourselves: the audacity of people on the outside to think their lives are anything like ours.

We say, "I'll start fresh." And that means nothing. Because we'll always have to say we were here first. But the jobs I had before aren't worth going back to. I console myself: even with a record I could wait tables again. Or maybe I could get a job at the Industrial Park, pruning shrubs maybe. Just to be outside.

Rachel's gone, though, and that asshole is playing electronic jazz now. And now I'll be awake until sunrise. I'll just draw myself to sleep.

Dr. Broome and I were trying to decide where to go. I was too embarrassed to let him see my mouse house. But on the other hand, I had to get Susan back home. So, we walked down the stairs to my apartment. By this time, Susan was content in the box, since she had clawed an escape hole. He'd put her collar back on, just in case.

"I can make you some supper," I said. "It's mostly vegetarian. I hope you don't mind."

"That sounds good. I mostly eat at The Wagon Wheel."

"Really?"

"Yeah. It's just easier. I don't cook much."

"I eat breakfast at Hardee's. Hot sausage sandwich, a cup of coffee. It's almost like a cafe. But not really. I cook veggie at home. I think the mice don't like it as much."

I tried to surreptitiously clean off the mice droppings from the counters. "Don't look," I said. "It's disgusting. It's why I got Susan. I was hoping she'd keep the mice at bay. And she did for a little while. It's just that since she's been sick, they've had a field day. Well, not a field day. I guess a house day. They always have field days..." I was sounding stupid. "Do you want a beer?"

Dr. Broome took the beer and sat at the table. I started peeling vegetables. I could make ratatouille at a moment's notice. The eggplant had some brown spots, but I cut them away. I had enough zucchini to make it passable. Fortunately, the mice hadn't eaten the cheese. Just setting Susan down, even with her funny cone hat, seemed to send them scurrying.

I opened a beer for myself. I had a vet in my house. I had almost lost my job. The mice had had the run of my house for the last few days. I put the water on to boil for the noodles. Those, the mice had gotten to.

"Who knew that mice liked noodles? I'm so sorry. I try to keep this stuff in the fridge."

"I can eat it without noodles."

"Really? This is going to be an awful meal. I'm sorry."

"It's better than what I usually make. Don't worry. Besides, enough beer, and we won't notice."

So, I managed to put together a semi-decent ratatouille. It was peculiar, but at least it wasn't mousy.

"How did you decide to be a vet, Dr. Broome?"

"Ed. Please. Not Dr. Broome. I grew up on a farm."

"It seems like it's more than that. I mean, you really like animals.
You even like Susan."

"Do I? No, I've always thought about animals. Since I was a kid.
Why we keep some. Why we live with some and not others.
"Why dogs and not dolphins?"

"Right. Or why we live with them at all. So, I ended up at Tuskegee.
It was practically the only place where you could get into vet school
if you were black."

"You know, I've never thought about it before," which was a lie,
and he knew it as I said it. "But I've never met another black vet." That
part wasn't a lie. I hadn't. But it was clear that I had thought about it
before. "Why did you settle in Johnsonville?"

"I had a wife here." He let it sit. I didn't pry. "We're divorced.
She moved. I stayed. I already had my practice. And the black folk
around here like having a black vet. Especially the farmers. They
don't trust the white guys as much. How about you?"

"What do you mean?"

"What on earth brought you to Johnsonville, North Carolina?"

"I wish I knew."

"Were you misinformed?"

"Partly. And partly, I had an idea in my head what it would be like.
I thought it would be more, well, idyllic."

By this time, we had finished our first beers. We were finishing
our food. I took the plates to the sink. "Sorry, but if I don't do the
dishes, the mice know they have a free meal. I think every mouse in
Johnsonville hears about it."

Ed stood up. "The least I can do is the dishes."

"Are you kidding? You saved my job tonight. Who knows what
Susan would have done? I won't have you doing my dishes. Just keep
me company while I work."

"Do you have any music?"

"No. It's funny, but I can't stand it when I'm home. I need silence.
I think I'm in the wrong field."

Ed laughed, and watched me do the dishes.

He spent only part of the night. I think he didn't want to be seen
with the white girl from the radio station. At least, he didn't want to
be talked about.

Sex with Ed was comfortable. I wasn't used to that. I had accepted
the frantic one-night stands with the activists who spoke on my
show or provided some actuality. At first I mistook Ed's slowness for
laziness, but then I realized that he simply liked to enjoy himself. I

didn't get tired of comparing our skin, even though it was probably a sexually hackneyed move. But what isn't?

Sometimes, afterward, Ed would smile and say, "This is what is right with the world. This is when you can appreciate everything. Even why we keep animals."

In fact, Ed never once spent the night, though he ate my rangy meals a lot and made use of my bed. It could have been race. Though it could have been age. As easy as it was to talk to him, I didn't bring that up. I did stop sleeping with my on-air guests.

Fall came, and more news of the chemical spill rattled into the station. More news of the gay cancer came through too, though there wasn't much new. Both stories seemed to repeat themselves until I was tired of reading them on air. And then suddenly, activists in the populated areas decided to do something about the chemical spill. Who knows what makes one story ignite and another story simmer?

The march was organized slowly. First were the environmental groups from Durham. Then the poverty groups from Raleigh. A few more non-profits trickled in their support. They settled on marching in Riverboro, a town that had also received its share of sludge, but was bigger than Johnsonville.

Riverboro was one of those towns that kept growing for no particular reason. Like weeds, some towns grow unbidden with no obvious economy to support them, no real sunlight or waters to feed them. And by the time it's the 20th century the towns were middling, without the connection to the bigger cities. The dry towns were small and compact, without the universities or research centers or industry other than old furniture mills or lumber yards or cotton mills. The old cotton mills, with their brown lung and cotton dust, rickety equipment on the verge of rusting out. Old loom fixers without teeth, waiting for pensions. The owners were just waiting for that last bale of cotton to spring forth, the last loom fixer to die, the last gear to rust into place before shipping the whole works off to China or Vietnam. No need to waste any of the equipment, no need to let any of it stand idle, but no need either to replace it when it just didn't make sense to use this labor force any more. Not that they paid union wages. The union was run out of town years before. But even regular wages were more expensive than the Asian wages, and so when that last bolt sprang off, the plan was for the whole organization to move.

At that point, the mill was still spinning thread. Polyester and cotton. Red this week. The dyes they used had long been pouring into the nearby Slader River, churning it brown or black, green and red alternately in the summers before a big Christmas order. But when people in Riverboro found out that other companies were pouring other chemicals, not from the cotton mill, but from an unknown chemical factory, there was an outcry across all class lines, across all race lines. It was one thing to pollute your own city for the greater good, but when another factory used your city for its own dumping, it was time to protest. Organizing was only slightly hampered by the fact that the culprits had yet to be found. It could have been one company or several. It could have been from a factory close by or up and down the east coast. It was clever actually, choosing to pollute the towns that had the fewest resources. They didn't have to worry too much about being caught, especially when the eye-witness was a drunk named Streeter. Still, the organizers seemed to hold out hope. I suppose they thought they could pressure some official into finding the invisible criminals.

The day turned out to be storybook sunny. Not humid, as it often was, and fortunately, not stinky the way the cotton mill sometimes made it.

Alice Johnson's grand-niece was there, in a green pretty dress. She carried balloons and sucked on a lollipop. Her mother carried a sign asking the world to be clean for her daughter, who was a fortunate prop.

Thad was there, trying to report live. Though, he always muttered under his breath that no one could tell the difference if he were reporting dead. His shoulder bag dug a groove across his shoulder, the weight of the cassette recorder dragging his right side to the ground. The recorder was a relic, the battery compartment held shut with duct tape, and the window on the front so scratched, it was opaque.

Rene was there, carrying the extra supplies Thad might need. Batteries and cables, cassettes and splicing tape. Rene carried lemonade in plastic jugs, and bologna sandwiches on white bread. They'd left Sasha with a friend, because Rene never took her child on marches, no matter how sunny the day or how benign the cause. Even now that Sasha was fourteen, it wasn't worth the risk to Rene.

A band started. A voice on a loudspeaker, disassociated from any body suddenly spoke. "This isn't Greensboro. This isn't Washington. This is little Riverboro. Speaking up for ourselves."

A few people in the crowd clapped, shouted. Most people were still assembling, waiting for buses from Raleigh and Durham. There were rumors that people were driving down from Washington and Richmond, but it seemed silly. Why would they bother? The march started out as these things do. People milled around, looking for their partners, looking for friends. High pitched feedback sounded over the PA system. Speakers gathered on the podium.

It wasn't clear that the sounds we heard were gunshots at first. And then almost everyone started screaming. Like dominos, we all hit the ground. After a minute we stood. It wasn't clear who had fired or what was going to happen next.

I saw that Ed was still on the ground. I ran over to him and screamed for an ambulance. There was blood everywhere, but Ed seemed unfazed. "I think it just grazed me," he said. Finally the ambulance arrived, scattering all the demonstrators. I don't know exactly what happened next, because I rode in the ambulance with Ed. I still can't believe they allowed me to go. They weren't supposed to. Or maybe I lied. I don't remember anymore.

The hospital in Riverboro was bright and gleaming. It was too shiny. Ed got patched up. He was right. It was just a graze, but he felt battered. We took a cab back to my car.

"You'll have to tell me how to get to your house," I told him. "Do you want me to stay?"

"No, thanks. But no. I don't want to talk much."

It didn't sound right, but I understood. As it turned out, women came out of the woodwork to bring Ed food and cater to him. I was the only white woman. I didn't bother to bring food.

We never did find out who was responsible for the chemical spills. But we did find out who fired the shots and why: an inexperienced trooper got nervous. That was it. Nothing dramatic, just life.

"So, it turned out to be a green cadet," I said to Ed.

"Sort of disappointing, isn't it? I can't really be a martyr for the cause, when it was just an accident."

The shooting carried WTPV for a few more weeks. There were news stories for us to file. That brought in a few dollars here and there. The shooting inspired a few more donors and a few new underwriters. But the grant that paid Marcus and me was running out, and Rene and Thad had depleted their savings. The new age of conservatism was quickly boxing us in.

Three months after the march, Thad and Rene called us together.

"The board met Sunday. We have to fold."

The announcement was brief and to the point. I don't think anyone was surprised. It was a simple statement. No one questioned it. There was no need. We had enough money to run the station for another month. And then it would be curtains.

The last month went quickly. We stopped asking for money on the air. No more "contributions from listeners" appeals. We announced the underwriters, even when they were no longer contributing, and we still read press releases from the area non-profits. We simply played jazz and of course blues. We hesitated to tell the listeners, but we thought it was only fair. Would they still listen if they knew our days were numbered? And that begged the questions: What if no one was listening? Does the sound just float into space? Is it saved somehow in some unseen pocket that we don't know about?

Shortly after the announcement, the transmitter jammed. Thad was in Raleigh, looking for work, so it fell on Rene and me to try to patch things up.

"We could just leave it," I said.

"Thad has had me climb the tower before."

"You don't sound too sure of yourself."

"I'm not. It's dangerous. But I don't want a screw-up to take us off the air early. I want to stay on for every goddamn minute we have left."

"I know, but we don't know what we're doing."

"I do, in a way. I'm supposed to make my way up the rungs without ever looking down, only looking across."

"Let's think about this," I said. "Maybe the transmitter will just unjam itself by magic."

"Or maybe we could fix it. Here," Rene said, reaching into her desk drawer. "Have some whiskey first. Then we'll decide."

We poured small shots. If we were going to climb the tower, we didn't want to be drunk. But we also didn't want to be completely sober.

Rene busied herself with the mail. I started pulling news stories, just in case we were successful or the transmitter fixed itself.

"Rachel. Look at this." Rene handed me a manila envelope with a return address from the prison.

There was a single sheet of notebook paper inside with a drawing of the four of us. It was remarkably accurate. I was pale. And the artist had cross-hatched color onto Thad and Rene and Marcus.

"Do you know this person, Rene?"

"No, she's not one of my interviewees. But she's a good artist. Though I don't think I really look that frenetic."

I couldn't tell her that she did. Just as I couldn't tell Marcus, had he been there, that he really looked that angry. I hoped that Thad would be amused to see himself tangled in wires and holding a screwdriver. I never pictured myself wearing the bewildered expression she gave me, but she placed me in an old Indian print skirt. I hadn't worn it in ages, but I was shocked someone could dress me just by the sound of my voice.

There was a brief note: *I'm sorry you won't be on the air anymore. I'll be getting out soon, but I would have missed you if I were still going to be in here. And by the way Rachel, don't be so serious.*

She'd signed her full name: Roberta Flowers.

"Okay." I shrugged. "Fuck it. Let's go."

"Okay, then. Let's go."

"Are you sure you can do this?"

"Yeah. Just look across. Not down. Climb the tower with my head up," Rene looked at the drawing again. "Am I really that frantic?"

"Yes. But it works. Let's go before we lose our nerve."

"You don't have to climb, but I'd like to know you were at the bottom, waiting for me."

"So I can break your fall?"

"Exactly."

So we packed up the tool box and headed over to the transmitter. We were quiet on the drive over. And when we saw the transmitter looming before us, we were both silenced by its size.

"I never thought I'd need to climb the tower by myself."

"You are making me very nervous."

The sky was starting to get dark by the time we unpacked the toolbox. Rene looked like she barely touched the rungs as she made her way up the transmitter. But I knew she was scared. Rene kept repeating, "This is Thad's job. Thad is the one that climbs the tower." I could see her resting on the ledge above. She had wires in her hands and was testing each connection.

In the distance a storm was starting to rumble.

"Rene, you need to hurry. I don't want you to get electrocuted."

"I don't want me to get electrocuted either. I think I see the problem."

"Good. Come down."

"In a minute."

The claps of thunder were getting closer. We needed to get electricity to the tower, but not in an electrical storm. We were too exposed. "Rene. Hurry."

In a minute I heard the cooling fans whir. Rene had restored the power. And even though we wouldn't need it much longer, it was important to hear it surging and to see the lights on the control panel light up.

Rene climbed down, just as the first crack of lightning burst the sky. I hugged her and shrieked, "I was so worried. I was so worried." The storm passed over us quickly. Just like at the march, we threw ourselves down on the ground, hoping not to attract the lightning. As suddenly as the storm appeared, it disappeared, and the sky brightened. Just as suddenly the sun dried the moisture, so it was almost impossible to tell that there had been a squall a few minutes before.

When we got back to the station, we apologized for the technical difficulties, avoiding the fact that in a couple weeks we'd be undone anyway. We just couldn't survive anymore, and the station had slowly starved to death. Rene and Thad took the last shift.

Afterward, I mourned a little. For the station, and for me and Ed. There was nothing for me in Johnsonville. So, I was curiously unencumbered. I left the poverty and the race issues behind. I stopped working in radio, had a child, gained weight. After I came to the conclusion that I simply wasn't good enough at radio, I was free to study other things. Oddly enough, I chose sales. It made sense. I had a good voice and people trusted me, which were my only useful qualities in radio. I miss news, though. It seems like the news is always coming at us. But just like back then, it's impossible to filter. What's important? Cats, AIDS, crows, SARS. However we find it, sometimes we spot the most important parts and sometimes we don't. The chemicals keep leaking into our lives. AIDS takes a back seat. Mostly I want news I can read; I can't listen to it.

A few days before we went off the air for good, I took a long walk back to the cow pasture where the transmitter stood. It was farther than I remembered, and by the time I reached the tower, I was tired. The tower stood starkly against the bright blue sky. It was hard to tell from here how much trouble we were in. I decided to rest under the tower. No storms were predicted. No heavy rain at this time. Just a light easterly wind. I lay on my back looking straight up into the tower, seeing how it narrowed to a peak in the sky. I could see the lights flashing, hear the fans whirring. Soon I would be leaving, and the tower would be silent. I shut my eyes. I fell asleep in the electricity.

MORE GREAT READS FROM BOOKTROPE

Deception Creek by **Terry Persun** (Coming-of-age Novel) Secrets from the past overtake a man who never knew his father. Will old wrongs destroy him, or will he rebuild his life?

Memoirs Aren't Fairytales by **Marni Mann** (Contemporary Fiction) Leaving her old life behind, Nicole finds herself falling deeper and deeper into heroin addiction. Can she ever find her way back to a life free of track marks? Does she even want to?

Devil in Disguise by **Heather Huffman** (Romantic Suspense) Reporter Rachel Cooper is America's Sweetheart—but that won't help her when human traffickers kidnap her sister. Can an old flame help her protect the ones she loves?

Spots Blind by **Linda Lavid** (Fiction – Short Stories) Stories about being blindsided—sometimes by family, friends, and lovers; sometimes by our own refusal to see the truth.

Summer of Government Cheese by **Paula Marie Coomer** (Fiction – Short Stories) A collection of darkly introspective short stories. As they say, one way to dispel darkness is to expose it to light.

… and many more!

Sample our books at:
www.booktrope.com

Learn more about our new approach to publishing at:
www.booktropepublishing.com

Made in the USA
Charleston, SC
16 April 2013